COMMANDO

Shoot To Kill

By

Peter Rische

Although it uses the general Rhodesian war situation within the time period it is set and is written in an autobiographical style, this book is a work of fiction. It does not make any attempt to replicate any actual Bush War postings or deployments of 3 Commando RLI. Further artistic licence had been used where the author thought it appropriate. All events pertaining directly to the author and the other featured characters are work of the author's imagination.

This book is written using British spelling and contains
Strong language.

On December the 6th 1978 it was my turn to join the bush war. I was eighteen years old. Unlike many of my contemporaries, I was a volunteer. With consent from my legal guardian, aged 17 and 7 months, I had joined the Rhodesian army some six months previously.

Although my parents were Rhodesian and I had been born there, I spent much of my early childhood in Malawi. My father was a successful businessman and had relocated to that country in order to oversee his numerous interests in the mineral extraction sector. For my part I was returned to Rhodesia to boarding school when I reached the minimum age requirement. As far as my parents were concerned my future had already been mapped out. School, university (possibly) then entrance into the family business, where I would serve an apprenticeship under my father before eventually taking the reins.

Unfortunately my parents were killed in a motoring accident when I was fifteen. I was an only child and passed into the legal care of an elderly aunt. With no one to administer it, the family business was broken up and sold off, as was my parents home and lands, with the money placed in trust for me.

I meant this as no disrespect to the wishes of my parents, but from an early age I knew I wanted to be a member of the Rhodesian Light Infantry. The RLI were the elite of the Rhodesian conventional fighting forces and they often found themselves at the epicentre of action of what had morphed from a low intensity insurgency conflict into a full scale war which spilled over into three countries.

Although my time was spent at boarding school, my aunt and I enjoyed a quite close relationship. She had no children of her own and had been widowed when her husband, who served as a pilot with the Royal Air Force in World War Two, was killed in action in Italy.

Auntie was most concerned when I announced my intention to join the army. Probably because of her personal experience, she was very much a pacifist by nature. She knew that I would be called up for military service anyway when I reached eighteen and had attempted to engineer events so that I could evade the draft. She tried her best to persuade me to move abroad or somehow have my call up deferred by entering into higher education. Despite her protestations, I was adamant that I wanted to help defend my country against the communist terrorist threat. Such was my resolve that she had no alternative but to bend to my will, signing the relevant paperwork which allowed me to join the army while still only seventeen.

Now, after a few army administrative oversights which almost saw me shunted off to another unit, and having passed the gruelling training course, I was posted to Three Commando.

The unit were operating from a former tourist resort called Hot Springs, in the north east of Rhodesia. I arrived at the Forward Operating Base (FOB) not knowing quite what to expect. Soon I found myself in front of my new Troop commander, a tall young Lieutenant by the name of Bentley. Lieutenant Bentley gave me a brief introduction to the mission which Three Commando were engaged and my responsibilities therein before sending me off to find the rest of the Troop. There was no 'welcome aboard' or handshakes (not that I'd been really expecting any), indeed quite the opposite. Bentley had been quite officious and rather curt, warning me to keep my ears and eyes open and my mouth shut whilst I learned the ropes from the other Troop members.

Three Commando was at Hot Springs on Fireforce duties. Give the fact that the Rhodesian military was only a small, permanently under strength force and that we were comprehensively outnumbered by our enemies, there was little prospect of our being able to successfully defend the borders of Rhodesia against terrorist incursion. Someone, somewhere, had come up with the idea of using small, yet highly mobile units of troops deployed directly into battle by either helicopter of parachute to get to grips with the enemy as and when they were discovered. This 'firefighting' method of combating the communist terrorist threat had proved highly effective, resulting in the elimination of countless enemies on Rhodesian soil for relatively little expenditure in manpower and effort.

In this particular instance, Three Commando was working with the helicopters of the Rhodesian Air Force (RhAF). Once the location of a terrorist unit had been identified, a helicopter borne mission would take place to attack and destroy them. It was hard, dangerous, immediate action work often conducted at close quarter. More often than not the attackers would be outnumbered and outgunned, yet utilising superior training and motivation, the Rhodesians were usually always successful.

Throughout my training the realisation that I was soon to be part of a full blown war had overtaken me. My desire to defend my country had been overshadowed by a deep and unsettling conundrum. Despite all that I was being conditioned to do; when shove came to push, would I really be able to kill someone? I don't know if other recruits had the same reservations as me because I never asked, but the sudden and very real prospect of having to take lives caused me many sleepless nights.

Here, at Hot Springs, I was soon to have my answer....

***

After only two days and having hardly time to settle into my new surroundings, on the morning of the 8th, we were mobilised.

We were on standby and were deployed close to the helicopters. The routine – such as I'd had chance to experience it – was simple. We would wait by the choppers until a call came in. I suppose it was a bit like those old films you see of Battle of Britain RAF fighter pilots waiting at their dispersal huts for the signal to scramble. If any terrorists were located the shout went out and, while the helicopters were going through hasty pre-flight procedures, we would assemble for a quick briefing as to the whereabouts of the enemy, their approximate strength and the lay of the land etc. It was bare bones stuff, just enough to equip us with the necessary information required to mount an attack. We would then emplane and as soon as the aircraft were ready, take off and make for the point of contact with all speed.

Unfortunately for us, Rhodesia had been subjected to tough sanctions for some years. This meant we could not import the military hardware necessary to conduct wider anti-terrorist operations. This, combined with our limited pool of manpower, put us at a distinct disadvantage. The only transport helicopters available in any numbers (albeit still restricted numbers) were the French made Alouette. These remarkable machines had proved their worth on countless occasions during the bush war. The main drawback was the fact they were light helicopters and were only capable of carrying two crew members and four fully equipped troops. Their restricted payload and – in the harsh high altitude environs of the Rhodesian bush – their restricted range, proved another limiting factor. The Alouette had been adapted to local requirements and, apart from the usual troop carrying 'G car' version, some had been modified to carry a sideways firing 20mm cannon. The 'K car' (Kill car) would provide close air support to ground troops. On many occasions where they were called in, the K cars could tip the balance of the fighting in the favour of outnumbered Rhodesian soldiers.

Here I was, scrambling aboard a G car with the other three members of my 'Stick'. The rotor blades wound up to capacity and we made a short rolling take off amid a whirlwind of dust.

Once airborne, I could see the other three G cars and the accompanying K car. It was going to be a big punch up, of that I had little doubt. The Terrorist gang had been located only twenty minutes flying time away. They were tracked down by one of our recce teams, holed up in the bush and blissfully unaware that death was about to visit them.

I had been trying my best to act relaxed yet alert during our periods of standby. I was aware that eyes were on me, scrutinising my behaviour and body language. The other blokes were completely justified in wanting to know who this skinny youth was and how he might react under fire. At the end of the day I wasn't only putting my own neck on the line, but I could easily endanger the lives of my comrades with any screw ups.

We were flying very low, not far above treetop height. The noise of the engines and the thud of the blades seemed to penetrate my very being. I tried to swallow but my mouth was far too dry. I suddenly realised I was sweating heavily and that one of the fast thumps was actually my own heartbeat. I chanced a glance at the others. They seemed tense yet somehow calm. I was forced to wipe the sweat away from my eyes with my forearm and noticed that the manoeuvre brought a couple of stares from the others. Was I going to fuck up?

Only minutes to go. The gooks may already have heard the approaching helicopters and would be coming to the alert. I was breathing hard through an open mouth and trembling slightly, whether or not this was fear or adrenalin or a combination of both, I had no idea.

The choppers landed with a bump and we were out into the maelstrom of dust. As quickly as they touched down they were airborne again, pulling away out of small arms range. My brain vaguely registered that there had been no gunfire. The enemy hadn't shot at our choppers and the door gunners hadn't opened up with their .30 machine guns.

As the din of the aircraft receded we had already formed up into a skirmish line. It was still early but already hot. The target area was a natural feature; a cross between a dry river bed and a re-entrant. It was about eighty metres wide with sloping banks at each side which rose in parts to about ten metres. Inside this feature we knew the enemy were lying in wait. It was quite close country, covered with a scattering of bushes and spindly trees. There was long grass and plenty of dead ground. Overall, it was ideal for defence, which didn't bode well for us.

Those we were after were a gang from the ZANLA terrorist army. ZANLA, led by Robert Mugabe, were based in Mozambique. Every last one of them were murderers. They showed no mercy to anyone. Black, white, young or old, men, women or children, they would kill without hesitation. These ZANLA scumbags had been responsible for visiting countless heinous crimes upon the black and white population of Rhodesia. They didn't restrict themselves to murder. They would (and did) happily torture and rape. Now it was time for a little payback....

Strangely, my nerves seemed to desert me and my training took over. I was still very much on edge, but not really scared any more. It sounds strange, and I can't fully explain it, but now I just wanted to get on with the job.

One Stick moved up to the left bank, another to the right, while my own and the final Stick spread out in five metre spacing line abreast across the bed of the depression. Slowly we began to move forwards. The hair on the back of my neck was standing proud and very fibre of my being was on high alert. I was listening and looking – even smelling – for the faintest sign of the enemy. We were moving through a very dense patch of chest high elephant grass. I could not see the men to my left or right. Was I going forward too quickly? Was I moving too slowly? Had the others stopped? Was I out in front on my own with no immediate support? Was I about to bump into the enemy?

All of a sudden battle was joined. The Stick on the left bank got into a sudden contact. There was a lot of fire, some of it automatic. I couldn't see what was happening. Bugger! What was I to do? I still couldn't see anyone to either side of me. Should I stop in the hope one of the others may emerge through the grass? No. My last orders had been to move through this area and close on the enemy. I guessed that the other blokes were still adhering to this so I could not be seen to let them down.

I was keeping my head down as I felt my way through the elephant grass, fearful of what I may be about to walk into.

Suddenly, close to my immediate front, a rifle opened up. It was firing rapidly on semi automatic. I stopped and crouched closer to the ground. 'What the fuck?' I had no idea what was happening. Looking to either side I still could not see anyone. 'Fuck! Fuck! Fuck!'

I noticed that some of the elephant grass was being cut down. This strange sight was accompanied by a weird 'whoosh' noise. It took only a fraction of a second for me to realise that someone was shooting into the grass in an attempt to flush us out. The bullets were scything the grass and the noise – I was astounded I could pick it out above the gunfire – was the sound of the grass being chopped. Using the grass as a marker, I saw that the bullets were closing in on my position.

Foolishly I popped my head up just above the grass to see what was happening and got the fright of my life when I saw a terrorist standing about ten metres away. Next to him was another gook who was only visible from the chin up. Standing man was firing an SKS rifle from the hip into where he thought we might be. I remember the look of surprise on his face when he saw me. His eyes came up like saucers (mine probably did too!) and we must have been as scared as each other. Immediately I saw him bring his weapon to bear. Even though I was shocked, I was too quick for him. I already had my rifle in my shoulder and ready to fire. It was one fluid move. I let him have it. At that range, even in my winded state, I couldn't miss. I must have fired three or four rounds and he dropped. There was no being thrown back off the feet like in the movies. He just went down and in that instant I realised why the guys referred to terrorists they shot as 'floppies'. Without hesitation I opened up on his mate, but by this time he was running away. I tried my best but I missed the bastard.

Suddenly the rest of the two Stick stood up and I realised that, yes, I had in fact got slightly ahead of them. As a group we moved forwards quickly until we found ourselves on the edge of a small depression within the floor of the basin in which the terrs (terrorists) had set up camp. There were bits of kit and a few bodies scattered about, but by now most of the enemy had run away towards the far end of the valley where the recce team and K car were waiting to ambush them.

Suddenly I saw a figure break cover and sprint across my front to the base of the right bank. He had an AK47 and fired a couple of wild bursts in our direction. I opened up on him and, when he was almost at the top of the bank, I hit him. He must have been killed instantly because he simply fell and slithered and half rolled back down the bank like a rag doll. Although I was absolutely convinced that I had got him, someone else claimed it was his shot which had taken the gook down. I didn't argue.

It was all over bar the shouting then. We swept the area but the terrs who had not been killed were now long gone, running for their lives back to Mozambique. After securing the site we searched the bodies and their equipment for intel. We recovered the weapons and ammunition for removal back to base. A couple of terrs had been found hiding in the undergrowth, They had been hit either by the assault teams or the stop group and decided to try and lay up then escape after we had left. They would be coming back with us then handed over to the police anti-terrorist people in Special Branch. No doubt the SB officers would be able to extract useful information.

All in all we had killed five terrorists, wounded several more and captured two. We had broken up a sizable enemy group (we estimated it to have been about twenty five strong) not long after they had infiltrated the border and before they had the opportunity to carry out terror attacks. We suffered no casualties. It was a good result.

Most important of all as far as I was concerned, was the fact that I'd slotted one (unofficially two) ZANLA thugs on my very first operation. I realised I had been worrying over nothing. The killing of the two terrs (I will always maintain that I shot the other one) had been easy. Yes it had been a knee jerk 'kill or be killed' thing, but I had neither hesitated nor felt any guilt afterwards.

I was perhaps getting a little ahead of myself when I thought I had proved my abilities. Little did I realise I had a long way to go. Still, I was on the right path….

***

Three days later we were back in action. This time our target was in Mozambique. Temporarily leaving our Fireforce duties at Hot Springs in the hands of the part time troops of the Territorial Force (TF), we had been moved as a Company to a nearby RhAF forward airfield (FAF). The rest of the Battalion were already ensconced at the airfield and as we arrived there was an air of expectancy about the place. Everyone had a theory as to why we had been assembled at such short notice, but the over-riding theme was that the Commandos of the RLI were about to conduct a large scale external Fireforce operation against Robert Mugabe's ZANLA. Operations of this nature were fairly commonplace and often utilised all available resources. One look at the activity within the FAF and it was obvious (even to a newbie like me) that things were going to get very hot, very soon….

Because of the small number of rotary wing aircraft available, it was often impractical in such circumstances to deploy troops by helicopter. As I mentioned earlier, the Alouette could only carry four men. Even if the RhAF could concentrate its chopper fleet together in one place for one operation, any attempt to move a significant force of soldiers would be both time consuming and tactically impractical.

The enemy, be they ZANLA or Joshua Nkomo's ZIPRA (who had their bases in neighbouring Zambia) had been subjected to enough camp attacks to know how they unfolded and how they could – possibly – be countered. The terrorists knew that their best defence was to run away, scattering to the four winds at the first sign of ground attack. The camps they used were often large and spread out across several square kilometres, thus making it more difficult for the attacking force to contain. To have piecemeal troop movements by helicopter presented the enemy with ample opportunity to escape.

The quickest and most effective way of deploying troops when conducting camp attacks (and in many instances 'normal' Fireforce missions) was to use parachute troops. A large enough force of men could be dropped to seal off the target before the terrorists had chance to react. Of course, we were battling with the fact that we never had enough men. Despite our best efforts, it was physically impossible to create an impenetrable ring around any camp; especially the larger ones, so some enemies were still bound to escape. However, this tactic meant we could catch as many as possible.

The Rhodesian Security Forces (RSF) boasted an unusually high proportion of parachute formations. As well as the SAS and Selous Scouts Special Forces outfits, there was the RLI and the Rhodesian African Rifles. The RAR was a Regiment comprised of black Rhodesians.

It was a very well regarded and highly effective unit, whose combat lineage could be traced back to the Far East theatres of WW2. I'm not sure of the dates, but the RAR was made parachute capable as the need for the rapid movement and deployment of troops became a necessity.

As for the RLI Commando Battalion, we were first inducted into the airborne brotherhood in about 1976. By the time I went through training at the RLI depot at Cranborne, Salisbury, the Regiment had been parachuting for two years. Throughout that time they had been pacesetting in the discipline. Often RLI troops on Fireforce duties could make operational jumps more than once a day, allowing them to quickly establish new world records for combat parachuting. Aside from the sheer number of descents, these same drops were often conducted at ultra low level. The reasoning was simple. It allowed the man to jump and deploy in the shortest time possible, thus cutting down the possibility of the terrorists to make good an escape. Jumping from low altitudes also reduced the risk of ground fire. In essence, as well as not having much time to shoot at the aircraft, the terrorists wouldn't be able to open fire at the parachutists themselves. Any military parachutists reading this will know the absolute minimum height requirements for it to be considered safe for a fully loaded soldier to jump. Well, I can report that the RSF in general often broke those rules. Dependent upon the situation, we would make our drops from 400 feet or even lower. At such low altitudes it was a question of just a few seconds between exiting the aircraft and hitting the dirt. The lowest officially recorded jump was made (in error I may add) at about 95 feet! Amazingly, everyone involved survived.

I never had any issues with parachuting; in fact I quite enjoyed the training 'fun' jumps. As a 'treat', these were sometimes conducted at a thousand feet to give the boys more time under the canopy.

Up to that time I had only completed my training jumps at the Parachute Training School at New Sarum airbase near Salisbury. I'd been awarded my wings then, after a short leave, bussed off to join my new company at Hot Springs.

Soon after our arrival at the FAF we were treated to a comprehensive briefing. As suspected, the target was a ZANLA training camp. The incumbent regime of Mozambique, an organisation known as FRELIMO (AKA 'Freddie' to us Rhodesians) were openly assisting Robert Mugabe in his quest to take control of our country. They allowed ZANLA free reign to organise, train and deploy its terrorist hordes. ZANLA would often concentrate his efforts, establishing training or holding camps which could in turn hold varying numbers of enemies, from hundreds to many thousands. Often, for the purposes of propaganda, these terror camps masqueraded under the guise of refugee camps, with ZANLA and FRELIMO declaring to the international community that they were home to persons displaced by war from Rhodesia. Each time they were hit roars of condemnation would ring around the globe. It mattered not to the world – and in particular the West – that the Rhodesians made careful appreciations of any camp before deciding to attack it. Many hours of careful ground reconnaissance work would go into building up complete pictures of suspected terror camps. Photographic evidence of military training at said camps would be released to the media in the aftermath of any raid, but photographs of 'refugees' carrying assault rifles while undertaking military drills was never enough to placate those who were dedicating themselves to turning Rhodesia over to the communists.

In this instance, the training camp was a recently established facility which, according to our intelligence people, could house up to two thousand trainees. Said would be terrorists were at various stages of training. Among the raw recruits, there were plenty of others who were almost ready for deployment. It was expected that we would encounter approximately fifteen hundred enemy. In total there were about 150 of us, including a detachment of SAS.

As an attacking force, being outnumbered fifteen to one isn't the best of starts. It would be almost impossible to effectively seal off the target, so we could expect large numbers of the enemy to successfully escape. We hoped to maximise our efforts by not only killing or otherwise incapacitating as many terrs as we were able, but then destroy the camp itself and everything in it. Our protocol of destroying abandoned materiel was a good way of denying the terrs valuable arms and equipment, equipment they could ill afford to lose. We could expect most of the recruits to drop their firearms and make a run for the safety of the bush as soon as they realised what was happening. We could expect it but not count on it. A fair proportion of the partially/fully trained ones may just feel like hanging round long enough for a fight.

As was often the routine in such training facilities, the day started early. The recruits would assemble and parade before dispersing to their various schedules. It was obvious that morning parade was the best time to strike if we were to maximise our chances of killing as many terrorists as possible. In this instance the attack would commence with an airstrike from RhAF Hunter jet aircraft. They would make a rapid low level pass over the parade ground as the terrorists were in mid flow, dropping 225kg bombs directly onto them. It was hoped that the high speed run would give the terrorists no warning and cause them to suffer heavy casualties as a result. The Hunters would then bank and make another pass, this time firing unguided air to ground rockets into the dispersing crowd. A third and final pass to strafe the area with 30mm cannon fire and they would be gone. Meanwhile the RhAF Dakota transport planes carrying the assault groups would be dropping us and the SAS. We'd be going in low; at 400 feet. Once on the ground we would form up and move forward in sweep lines towards the camp. It was our intention to get into contacts with as many terrorists as possible as they attempted to flee the scene. Once at the camp itself, we would fight our way through before finally securing and searching it. We would be looking for classified documentation or anything else of potential intelligence value.

Something as innocuous as a discarded camera could hold a roll of film which, when developed, may be of interest to the intelligence people, or further proof as to the true nature of 'refugee' camps. Sometimes the terrorists would build heavily disguised underground spaces in which they would store secret material or hide themselves. Therefore it was always necessary to be thorough when conducting searches. All the weapons, ammunition and other ordnance would be piled up and destroyed by fire or explosion. The same fate would befall the buildings, any vehicles and items of personal equipment. It was our intention to deny the terrorists anything which may be of value to them.

The operation was scheduled to commence at dawn the following day. The intervening period was spent preparing our weapons and equipment. I admit to not sleeping much because I was apprehensive about how the following day would unfold. 1500 terrorists and 150 of us? Even if our briefing officers expected the bulk of them to melt away into the bush, we'd still be outnumbered.

In the early hours we were roused to begin our final preparations. Weapons and kit were double checked, 'chutes were drawn and we assembled by the aircraft. We were given the usual warning that failure to jump would result in court marshal before being helped up the steps and into the Dakota. Despite the fact that the operation was scheduled to end before last light, every man was heavily loaded with a rifle or a machine gun and lots of spare ammunition. There was little prospect of resupply once we were on the ground so none of us took any chances, carrying as much as we were able.

It was still dark when our small flotilla of ParaDaks took to the air. In terms of flying time, we were about forty minutes from the target. No one spoke much; you couldn't be heard above the noise of the two massive radial engines anyway. I tried to concentrate on the forthcoming jump. When parachuting from a Dakota you had to observe certain rules. I suppose it's much the same for other types of aircraft, but seeing as I only ever jumped from the Dak I always deemed it aircraft specific. Upon exiting the 'plane you had to present as small a cross section as possible. This was because you would immediately be caught in the prop wash and slipstream. To jump with arms or legs flailing would send you into a tumble from which it was all but impossible to recover. Jumping at the ultra low altitudes we did meant almost certain death if you didn't go out clean. I repeated over and over inside my head that it was vital that I jump correctly. Arms crossed on top of the reserve 'chute, legs together and present a sort of 'at attention' pose. As soon as I felt the canopy deploy I would have only seconds with which to go through the rest of the routines. Check the canopy, check all round to make sure I wasn't about to collide with anyone or they with me. Finally look below. If clear I could release my pack. It would fall away to dangle on a paracord about ten metres long. Given the fact that we were fully loaded meant we would descend a lot quicker than a normal parachutist. The pack would hit the ground first and the sudden removal of its weight from the equation would cause the parachute to decelerate just enough to allow a safe landing. That was the theory anyway. From leaving the plane to hitting the ground would take about ten seconds. Not much time to get it right!

At the amber light we were up and checking our own and the man in fronts 'chutes. The din from the engine and the rattle of shudder of the airframe conspired to overwhelm the senses. We were flying through hot air and it was a bumpy ride. I clung tightly onto the strop in order to steady myself. Green light on 'GO'. We shuffled forwards. I saw men disappear through the portside door. Then it was my turn. The dispatcher was just a blur. I was out, eyes closed, and fell until I my descent was checked by a massive gut wrenching jerk on my harness. Eyes open now. Canopies everywhere. My own had opened properly. More panic as I saw the ground leaping up to meet me. Release the pack. Prepare for landing. Knees and feet together. Legs slightly bent. Elbows in. CRASH! God almighty! I had gone in forwards and hit the dirt hard. I was on my back now and struggling with my harness.

As the roar of aero engines receded it was overtaken by the sound of gunfire and explosions then the sudden shriek of jet engines. The Hunters were making their second pass, raking the target with high explosive rockets.

I was up, gathering my 'chute. I had retrieved my pack and hauled it onto my back. The parachute would be left where it was for now. It and all the others would be recovered later on. Another low level pass and the thump of large calibre cannon. The jets were strafing the terrorists as they ran. The Hunters would be turning for home now. The rest was up to us....

To my front, above the spindly trees and assorted vegetation, several columns of black smoke were rising into the morning sky. I joined the others in the skirmish line and together we began to press slowly forwards. There seemed to be shooting at points both near and far but none of it close enough for me to participate in. I had to be extra careful now. The terrs who had survived the airstrike were scattered and some of them would be coming our way. At ground level the vegetation was such that it was difficult to see in excess of thirty metres in any direction. I could easily walk into someone coming the other way. The terrorists would be so desperate to escape the encirclement that they would fight their way through our thin line. It was vital that we saw them before they saw us.

By now the familiar rattle of rotor blades rent the air. Several predatory K cars were stalking the area, plugging the gaps and hoping to catch the enemy out in the open. Every now and then short bursts of 20mm cannon fire rolled through the bush as the K cars spotted their prey.

Onwards we pressed. I was straining to look into the bush but spotted no movement. The sound of contacts continued to reach my ears but still I encountered nothing.

Eventually, and without firing a shot, I and the rest of my troop came upon the edge of the training camp. While there was still some shooting, the bulk of it had already passed. It was obvious to me that many of the terrorists had managed to make good their escape. Unfortunately that was one of the penalties of making such an attack with an under strength force.

The camp itself appeared deserted. A K car whooshed in above us as if to scout the place. It quickly banked then went off in search of trade elsewhere.

Some of the long grass around the camp had caught fire and smoke from that and several smouldering huts billowed across the scene. We were out of cover now and moving through the open areas of the camp proper. The bombs and rockets had done their work. Blackened craters adorned the site and the bodies which were scattered about told their own story of a successful RhAF airstrike. Mixed in amongst the detritus of what ZANLA would no doubt claim was a refugee camp were lots of rifles. Caught unawares in the middle of morning parade the 'refugees' had simply discarded their weapons and ran.

That day was the first time I had ever seen a dead body and it was a baptism of fire. It seemed that many of the dead had been caught up directly in the bomb and rocket blasts, the shrapnel visiting gruesome injuries upon them. Limbs had become detached from bodies, guts torn apart or heads split open. I vividly remember one man who had the back of his skull missing and both eyes popped out onto his cheeks. Each time I see those comedy spectacles with eyeballs on springs, I am always reminded of that.

Although I must admit to having my stomach turned by some of the sights, I had no sympathy for the recipients of the RhAF attack. They were common murderers. Had they been given the opportunity, they would have entered Rhodesia to kill, mutilate and rape members of the civilian population. By dispatching them, we had saved some of our own people from a terrible fate.

After about three hours the camp and the whole area surrounding it had been cleared and secured. We were pushed out onto the perimeter to protect against possible counter attack, while other teams searched the camp and prepared the captured ordnance for demolition.

Before long the camp was set ablaze. Recovered arms and ammunition had been thrown into some of the buildings then those buildings set alight. More smoke drifted across the bush, accompanied by the sporadic crackle of exploding bullets....

Our withdrawal began when a clutch of G cars came in. Our parachutes were too precious to leave behind so they too were to be recovered and removed back to Rhodesia.

My Stick was among the first to board the choppers and we found ourselves flying at low level back home. I can't really say that after all the build up, the raid had been a personal anti-climax for me because I wasn't sure if I was relieved or disappointed that I had no opportunity to get to grips with the terrorists. All I knew for certain was that I was dripping with sweat, my uniform was caked in dust and smelled of smoke and that I hadn't fired my rifle all day long....

Later, when reports of the raid began to filter down to us, we learned that it had been a bad day for ZANLA. Some eighty five terrorists were confirmed killed and an unknown number wounded. One senior officer had been captured and a sizable number of small arms and a quantity of ammunition destroyed. The camp itself was razed to the ground and along with it personal equipment, uniforms, boots and such. A cache of landmines along with several vehicles were also blown up.

Frustratingly, the bulk of the ZANLA trainees had escaped. Again this was due entirely to the fact that we had deployed in insufficient numbers and were unable to effectively seal off the target.

As for ourselves, our casualties ran to two men wounded.

We had displaced a large body of terrorist trainees and destroyed an important facility. The results could have been much better but our limited resources had dictated the outcome.

For me personally, I could now add my first operational jump to my parachute logbook.

***

We returned to Hot Springs to learn that during our absence ZANLA terrorists had hit a farm about 40ks west of our base. They had killed or driven off the black workers and murdered the farmer, his wife and their two children before burning the house and surrounding buildings to the ground.

The savagery of the terrorist knew no bounds, and this latest example of barbarity left me with both a feeling of revulsion and determination, a determination to do my best to stop these ZANLA scum….

The TF soldiers had deployed to follow up the terrorists, but the perpetrators simply melted into the depths of the bush to regroup and strike again somewhere else.

Apart from the occasional mortar attack, the gooks would never attempt to attack a security forces base. They were far too cowardly for that. They restricted themselves at all times to soft targets, targets which couldn't really fight back. That said, and knowing they were at the top of the terrorist hit list, the farming communities across Rhodesia mobilised their own meagre resources in order to defend themselves and their properties. They were allowed to own military grade firearms and as such weren't entirely toothless. The farmers also organised themselves into mobile patrols so they could react to attacks upon each other's farms. Being Rhodesian, the civilians were very inventive. They made improvised armoured vehicles; light flat bed trucks with homemade cupolas mounted on the back. Inside the cupola would be a farmer armed with a light machinegun!

The more prosperous farmers could supplement whatever local defence was available to him by hiring armed security guards. These guards were also armed with assault rifles.

However, and despite their best efforts, the ZANLA and ZIPRA terrorists kept coming....

***

On Christmas Eve 1978 we received a warning order for a move to another Forward Operating Base. Such a move meant only one thing; another external mission was imminent.

When we arrived we were briefed by an SAS Captain. As already guessed, the job was an external into Mozambique. Even though the target was a priority, the job was to be a small scale one. Two Troops from Three Commando were to provide support for an SAS operation in the Zambezi valley.

The SAS had been active in that part of Mozambique for some time and it had come to their attention that ZANLA were using a particular bridge as a main supply route between their rear area and forward bases. According to the Captain, the terrorists had been putting a lot of Rhodesia bound men and equipment across it. The SAS had received approval to destroy the bridge but there were a lot of enemy in the vicinity. Both ZANLA and 'Freddie' FRELIMO was stationed quite close to the target bridge. The SAS rightly presumed that neither would be content to allow a party of Rhodesians to just stroll in and blow up such an important bridge. So, while the SAS demolition teams went about their task, it would be our job to protect them.

At dawn on Christmas Day, we were airborne and heading for the big river. It took us an hour to reach the target area and the ParaDaks flew at low level all the way. We knew that Freddie had AA weapons stationed in the area but we were not fired upon as we made our final approach to the DZ. We jumped at low level and made it down without incident.

My Troop had been landed north of the river, about 500 metres from the bridge. The DZ was small, but the aircrew had placed us right on top of it. We formed up and quickly made for the location from which we would mount our defence. The small scrap of high ground about 250 metres away from the span gave us a commanding view in all directions. We could see the road which led away north and knew this was the quickest and easiest route with which the enemy could arrive on the scene. If they did, then they would soon discover that we were blocking the way to the bridge....

By this time the other Troop and the SAS had landed on the southern side of the river. The SAS quickly dispatched the small FRELIMO guard detail assigned to protect it. Even as we were digging in the SAS were setting to work on the bridge.

At this point the river was quite wide, so it goes without saying the span was a long one. It was a modern concrete and steel structure built, I believe, with Western aid money. For the SAS, the job of destroying the bridge was not as simple as some may first imagine. For this task a detailed survey of the bridge had already been carried out by an SAS covert recce team. They wanted to identify how the bridge was built so they could plan how best to attack it. The SAS back in Rhodesia would have worked out a demolition plan, a blueprint from which the demolition team would work. Explosives – the minimum amount of explosives as calculated by the experts – would be placed at critical points along the bridge. Once the charges had been laid and looped together on a detonation ring main, the resulting explosions would cause structural failure and collapse. It was hard, time consuming work.

About two hours after our arrival, we watched as a mechanised column of FRELIMO appeared along the highway. They advanced through the heat haze and stopped about 600 metres short of our position. Freddie was already aware of the pair of RhAF Hunters circling high above the scene but he didn't know where the Rhodesians had sited their ground protection troops. I could see Freddie quite clearly. He had a few Russian made APCs and at least one AA gun mounted on the back of a flatbed lorry. The troops were all riding in trucks. I guessed that there was at least a Company's worth of infantry and a dozen or more vehicles.

As the troops began to dismount our Forward Air Controller asked the Hunter pilots to make a warning pass. One of the aircraft banked and came screaming over our heads towards the enemy. The intention was not to open fire but to scare Freddie into inaction with the threat of an airstrike. However, as the Hunter passed low over their heads, some of the Freddie's opened up with rifles. It was only the speed of the Hunter which saved it from damage as it screamed back up into the sky. The fact that the aircraft had been attacked sealed Freddie's fate. The second Hunter was informed that FRELIMO were shooting. It too fell earthwards towards the enemy but this time it loosed its rockets. The noise of the jet engines and the explosions was terrific. Whoever the pilot was, he was a good shot, putting a cluster of HE rockets directly into the FRELIMO column. As the Hunters assumed their position in the sky above us the smoke and dust had settled enough for us to see the results. The second Hunter had really knocked the shit out of the enemy. I could see that one of the APCs was on fire, as were three or four of the trucks. Freddie appeared to have scattered into the brush on either side of the road. They were too far away for us to engage (we couldn't see them anyway) so we just settled back to wait....

Soon the Hunters left the scene, returning to Rhodesia to re-fuel and re-arm. The small gap in our defences between their exit and the arrival of two other aircraft was felt at ground level. We had no back up now and Freddie had a small time frame in which to exploit the fact....

As if on cue, no sooner than the Hunters had left the scene, a party of FRELIMO appeared about 200 metres to our front. They were moving in extended line and working their way tentatively forward in the knowledge that Rhodesian troops were out there somewhere to their front waiting to open fire.

We let them come on and when they were about one hundred metres away, we opened up. They retreated faster than they had come, melting back into the undergrowth. I don't think we hit anyone, I certainly didn't, but we did scare them. However, by initiating the contact, we had now given away our own position.

Not long afterwards the second pair of Hunters arrived. The Freddie AA gun opened up as soon as it saw them, 23mm tracer shells going skywards in longish inaccurate bursts. Without further ado, one of the Hunters swooped and dropped two 225kg bombs. I felt the concussion of the explosions. I presume the AA gun had been put out of action because it didn't fire after that.

By now it was mid afternoon. We had seen no more of Freddie since our last contact. The SAS were still hard at work preparing the bridge for demolition. Some people may ask why the RhAF didn't just come along and bomb it, thus saving all the time and effort and potential danger to Rhodesian troops? For a start we didn't have 'smart' laser guided bombs like the ones available today. Although I'm no authority, I am aware that a bridge presents a difficult target for an aircraft. Any hits were likely to be proximity hits and the damage caused relatively easy and quick to repair. Using specialists on the ground, the destruction of the target would be complete and virtually assured. The SAS would drop the span and put the bridge out of action for many months, if not indefinitely. The nearest crossing was about sixty kilometres away, thus the removal of this bridge would create great difficulties for the ZANLA logistics chain. That's why its destruction was so important.

A little while later we received word from the Hunters that a large formation of enemy was moving towards us through the bush at about two kilometres distance. The Hunters reported that they appeared to be FRELIMO of Battalion strength and were being supported by light armour.

This was bad news. Our protection group comprised sixteen men. Now Freddie was closing on us with four hundred or more troops! Upon arrival at our position I had dug myself in behind a couple of large rocks. I had a good angle of fire and view and could easily cover my arcs, all the while being afforded good hard cover. I reckoned I was going to need every scrap of help I could get so dug myself in a little deeper. Aside from our FN rifles, we had two MAG GPMGs. Our officer had insisted that we supplement our firepower by having two of the men swap rifles for Russian made RPD light machineguns. These weapons weren't standard issue, they had been recovered from terrorists and distributed among the RSF for use against their former owners. They were good weapons, able to withstand abuse and neglect yet still keep firing. With a pair of MAGs and two RPDs the fire effect of our little band would be substantially increased. To an enemy, it would seem that he was facing a larger force than was actually the case. Given the fact that we were being closed upon by an overwhelmingly numerically superior force, this bit of subterfuge may well just save our necks….

Knowing exactly how small in number we were and fearful of the outcome should the enemy get within range of our position, the Hunters made a pre-emptive strike on the advancing FRELIMO. A clutch of 225kg bombs were dropped and this was followed up by two low level strafing runs. From my point of view the action served to pinpoint the location of the enemy. They were still far away, but close enough to threaten us within a relatively short space of time.

Their ordnance spent, the Hunters retired to Rhodesia. The hole they had left would soon be filled but until that time, we were once again on our own.

We prepared for the worst. All eyes were scanning arcs in search of movement. Aside from the main force of FRELIMO, there were still the ones we had shot up earlier. Where were they and what were they up to? Up to about 120 metres from our location, Freddie would have cover enough to close on us without being seen. At any moment we were expecting them to emerge and charge forward. Perhaps though they were content to keep us under observation until their reinforcements arrived? Although we didn't know where they were, they knew we were dug into this little bit of high ground. Once the main force arrived they could stand off and saturate us with machine gun and cannon fire before making an infantry assault to take our position. Hurry up RhAF!

Presently another pair of Hunters appeared and took up station several thousand feet above us. Also, surprisingly, two Lynx aircraft also made an entrance. The Lynx was a light ground attack aircraft with a twin boom fuselage and push/pull propeller setup. They were used by the RhAF in several roles, including close air support. For this duty they mounted a variety of light weapons, from machine guns to small calibre rockets and bombs. The Lynx had proved a tough and capable aircraft and was always a welcome sight over the battlefield. Acting on the reports of the previous Hunters, the RhAF had dispatched two Lynx's to the scene. They flew in a wide orbit, lower than the Hunters, to act as a visual deterrent to the unseen FRELIMO….

Thankfully, the expected FRELIMO attack never materialised. Seeing our aircraft circling like vultures waiting to pounce, Freddie must have realised that he didn't fancy dying on Christmas Day, melting into the embrace of the bush to fight another day.

Eventually, about eleven hours after we landed, the bridge was finally ready. We withdrew across it and onto the southern side. We were the last people who would ever be travelling over that particular bridge. One of the SAS team blew an air horn. This was the pre-arranged signal to let us know there was going to be an explosion. I was expecting a massive earth shaking eruption and lumps of concrete to come raining down all over the place, but the actual explosion was quite muffled. The SAS had done their job well. The entire span had been surgically removed from its supports and gone crashing down into the water. The piers themselves had also been attacked and damaged beyond repair.

We were lifted by helicopter in several waves and returned to Rhodesia. It had been a good day. We had removed a vital link in the terrorist supply chain and had suffered no casualties whilst doing so. FRELIMO on the other hand had some men killed and an armoured car, AA gun and a few soft skinned trucks destroyed.

For ZANLA, the loss of the bridge would be keenly felt over the coming months. The inconvenience of re-routing traffic would have an instant and detrimental effect upon their supply efforts.

Yes, it had been a job well done. Upon our return to the FOB we enjoyed a late Christmas lunch and several celebratory beers.

***

The next week or so was quiet. We returned to Fireforce duty at Hot Springs but found ourselves unemployed. The lull in terrorist activity was unusual – though not unwelcomed. We filled our time by sitting close to the choppers and playing cards, or ball games, or working out on the collection of gym equipment which had been set up for the task.

I found I was fitting in well with my Troop. On the whole they were a friendly bunch. I hoped my performance thus far had been enough to gain their trust, or at least lose their suspicions of a wet behind the ears recruit….

***

Only a few days into the New Year we got the order to move. A large ZANLA gang had been tracked down by one of our recce teams and were holed up in the hills north of the town of Umtali. They had probably come over the border from Mozambique in small groups before rendezvousing at this location prior to mounting a big attack somewhere further in country. As I recall we were told there were approximately sixty terrorists in the group, making it an unusually large target. Our own troop availability was somewhat more modest. We had twenty four men available, plus a couple of K cars and the four man recce callsign. As always, our operations were dictated by lack of helicopters. In order to get us to the target in one move we were to parachute into the target area.

I was getting used to the routines by now and this one followed the same familiar pattern. After the briefing we boarded the aircraft and set off. My memory is a little hazy but I believe it took us about 30 minutes to reach the target.

The run in was as I expected. The ParaDaks came in low and we parted company at about 350 feet. The enemy would have heard our aircraft before we arrived and known we were coming to attack them. Usually that would have been their cue to scatter, this time though, it seemed that they had confidence in their own numbers....

We deployed into a skirmish line and began to move forwards at walking pace. Both K cars were circling the immediate area, waiting to catch the terrorists out in the open as they fled the scene. The ground between us was quite close; by that I mean there were lots of vegetation and points of cover making it difficult to see or indeed be seen.

All of a sudden, from a low lying ridge about forty metres to our front, the enemy opened up on us. They had at least two LMGs plus semi automatic rifles. They were well dug in and, as such, had the advantage. All around us bullets were striking trees, cutting vegetation and raising clouds of dust as they slammed into the bone dry earth. We got down and replied. Because of the dense nature of the bush it was difficult to see ahead properly. When you can't see anyone you don't know where to shoot. Shooting for the sake of it is not only a waste of ammo, but a sure fire way of giving away your own position and getting shot at in return. Initially I didn't fire. I was looking for muzzle flashes. When you see a muzzle flash in front of you it becomes your point of aim, because behind the flash is the man doing the shooting. Within a second or two I had seen what I was looking for. Fighting the urge to open fire, I aimed my rifle. I only fired one shot. Whether or not I hit anyone I don't know, but I saw no more shooting from that particular point.

By this time battle had been well and truly joined, the terrorist positions were being raked by sustained rifle and MAG fire. I fired several rounds at another target. Again I don't know if I hit anyone. At the command we began to close. Under covering fire from one group, the other charged forwards for ten metres before stopping and opening fire. The first group then made their own move. This leapfrogging meant we could rapidly close on the enemy while enjoying supporting fire all the way. I was part of the team who made it to the bottom of the ridge during their bound. Fire was being concentrated on the terrorist positions by the others, but the gooks were standing their ground and replying in kind. We couldn't call in the K cars because we were now too close to the gooks. One of the terrs threw a grenade which exploded harmlessly among the rocks.

The ridge was about fifteen metres high and the slope leading to it quite steep and strewn with boulders. Looking about I saw an NCO hand signal for us to go up it. Although the support group were doing a good job of suppressing the enemy, we were still being subjected to some heavy fire as we ascended the slope. I remember a couple of incoming rounds twanging off a rock as I was passing it. Some bastard was shooting at me! I dived for cover then felt at my chest webbing. I extracted a grenade and hurled it as hard as I was able up towards the top of the ridge. I heard it explode somewhere beyond the ridgeline then sent my second (and last) grenade in pursuit. I was up again and scrambling upslope. As I reached the top some of the others had made it before me. The terrs had already retreated, leaving a few dead and wounded behind.

The ground to our front was fairly flat and devoid of any real cover or dead ground. It ran for about thirty metres before rising up into the scrub covered hillside beyond.

There seemed to be a curious lull in proceedings at that point. We were waiting for the other troops to join us and the terrs just stopped firing. However, the ceasefire wasn't to last. As soon as the rest of the group had joined us and got into position to provide fire support we were ordered across the little plateau. It was only thirty metres but by got it seemed like thirty light years. The usual ten metre bound was out of the question as there was no place for us to get into cover, and the terrs could simply fire down from their positions on the hillside into us.

As soon as we began the assault we became the focus of heavy incoming fire. It was all a slow motion blur. I remember running, not shooting, and looking for a point to seek some cover. Angry balls of metal were buzzing by my ears. I could see the earth erupting in plumes of dust. A green firefly came from nowhere at a million miles an hour, hitting the dirt then bouncing off and going straight between my legs. Green tracer! Bastard! It almost took off my balls! Onwards I sprinted. I was breathing hard through an open mouth. At last, after what seemed like an age, I found myself at the far edge of the little plateau and immediately flung myself down into the nearest scrap of cover. We're getting fucking murdered here! Weapon up! Shoot! Aim at the muzzle flashes! The problem was I could see no muzzle flashes! I could see nothing. Bullets were still striking the ground around me, but I guessed the bulk of fire would now be being directed against the rest of the team as they made to run across the open ground. It was all very confusing.

Without knowing what I was shooting at, I simply opened fire, putting rounds up towards where I thought the enemy was hiding in the hope of suppressing them. Any time now the others would be running to join us, dodging the incoming hailstorm of bullets. They wouldn't leapfrog this time, instead go firm on our positions before we began the climb up the hill as one force. Vaguely I recall hearing the bass thump of twenty millimetre cannon fire. The K cars had joined in the fight. HE rounds were slamming into the hillside against places I could not yet see.

As I was changing my magazine something – I'll never know what – made me half roll then look back. Behind me and only a few paces away was one of my friends. I had become matey with him soon after joining the Troop. He was a good solid ouen, only slightly older than me and a man you could depend on. Everything still seemed to be playing out in slow motion. I shouted at him to get down into cover. He looked me straight in the eye. At that exact second he was hit, knocked down by a burst of automatic fire. I put my head down as another burst came looking for me. I had to get my mate into cover. I couldn't shoot now anyway because the others were on their way up the hill. I crawled out the couple or three metres to where he lay and, taking hold of his feet I dragged him into the side of the slope. Incoming rounds were still landing thick and fast. I could see blood on my mate's chest. He appeared to be still breathing. I got beside him and started talking. I told him to hang on and that everything was going to be okay. I was searching for his morphine syringe. My intention was to administer it. I had shouted for the medic but got no response. I simply couldn't be heard about the gunfire. From the blood I guessed that he had taken a round through the lung. I would roll him onto his side to stop him drowning in his own blood. Where was that bloody syringe? We all kept them in the same place so that we could quickly find them. It wasn't there. I went for his helmet. I knew some blokes carried a spare in the lining. Unfastening his chinstrap I could see he was staring at the sky and his eyes were flickering. I did my best to reassure him. As I removed his helmet his brains spilled out onto the ground. In my haste I didn't notice that a round had gone through his helmet. It had taken the back of his head off.

I can't begin to describe in detail how I felt. I felt sick, I felt guilty, and I felt angry. There was nothing for me to do but leave him. The rest of the Troop was now moving up the slope and there was no way I could leave a hole in the line. If I did then I would be endangering someone else. I remember shouting at the bloke to my right to tell him that *** had been killed.

I know it sounds callous, but you simply push things out of your mind at the time. When you yourself are being shot at, the self preservation instinct kicks, your training takes over and you just get on with it. However, that particular incident has stayed with me ever since. There's not a day goes by when I don't think about it. It also visits me in my sleep, the nightmare replaying itself in graphic detail. I blame myself for finishing him off by removing his helmet. The fact that he was already dead and what I thought were signs of life were probably the twitchings of the nervous system doesn't help much.

Like I said, at the time I just carried on with the task. We continued up the slope, shooting at anything which moved. Within a matter of minutes the terrs broke and ran. I spotted one in open ground and shot him dead.

The shooting subsided as quickly as it began. We continued forward, sweeping the bush to try and pick up the enemy again but they had gone.

It took a couple of hours or so to secure the area conduct our follow up. Some of the terrorists had run into to the recce callsign stop group and been shot up. Others had been spotted from the air by the K cars and treated to some more cannon fire.

In this action we accounted for seven dead and an unknown number wounded. We had broken up a large terrorist gang before they had chance to carry out any attacks. They were now split and running for the Mozambique border. Follow up units were dispatched in order to stop them from reaching it. Sadly we had lost one man dead and another seriously wounded. My friend would be sadly missed and his loss ensured our victory was pyrrhic.

It was early afternoon before we were stood down. As we waited for the G cars to arrive and begin airlifting us out in half Troop increments, what I'd experienced with *** really hit me. I had to sit down or I would have simply collapsed where I stood. All the energy drained out of me. I was sweating like hell and how I wasn't sick I'll never know. I was completely out of it for about five minutes and some of the guys thought I had gone down with dehydration. Slowly my strength returned. It was delayed shock, a shock so severe it shut down my systems. The shock of seeing a friend killed in the most terrible circumstance and, if I'm being honest, the shock of surviving several close encounters myself.

We went to *** funeral thc ncxt week. He was buried with full military honours in Salisbury. The Troop (including his replacement) fired a salute over his grave. I was glad to get back to base....

***

January 1979 saw things really hot up. Both terrorist armies were pouring men across the border from Mozambique and Zambia. Our intelligence people estimated that there were approximately 25,000 ZANLA and ZIPRA terrorists in Rhodesia at any one time. Given our own meagre resources in terms of both men and material, we had little answer to the frequency and scale of these incursions.

We relied heavily on our reserve units and Territorial Force soldiers became liable for ever longer periods of active service. The situation became such that an auxiliary reserve programme was initiated, which took in men who were otherwise too old to fight. Now, Rhodesian males up to and including the age of sixty found themselves being mobilised for security duties in urban areas.

Overall, the situation was dire. Massively outnumbered and outgunned, the Rhodesians chose to continue the struggle against communist terrorism. In the wider context of the cold war, it remains a mystery to me why Britain and the US were so keen to stand idly by and allow one of the most prosperous nations on the continent of Africa to be taken over by Soviet or Chinese inspired communist terror groups. Britain's reasons were obvious, but the stance of the USA, aside from acting in support of its ally, were less clear.

***

In order to overcome some of our deficiencies in terms of lack of men and equipment, clever workarounds were often employed. Fireforce had proved a tremendous success, with countless thousands of terrorists being killed during external missions in Zambia and Mozambique. Within Rhodesia it was no less successful. One contributing factor, indeed a vital component, was the use of small teams of men whose task was to be inserted into remote areas to carry out reconnaissance and tracking patrols. Working inside, yet parallel to the border, these teams would patrol in the hope of picking up signs of movement by the terrorists as they crossed into Rhodesia. Each team would include at least one man who was an expert in tracking. Once 'spoor' had been found HQ would be notified then the team would follow it up until it led to the enemy. At that point a Fireforce mission could be initiated. Usually the recce team would take part in the attack by acting as a stop group, laying in wait to ambush any terrs who managed to escape the main assault.

It was a dangerous job. The recce team would be far away from support and lacked the firepower to deal with any terrorist group who they encountered. For their part, the terrs knew of this tactic and had taken to utilising their own countermeasures. They would sometimes leave men behind the hope of ambushing the recce team as they followed their trail. They may also spike said trail with concealed booby traps.

The recce team would also have to carry all the equipment required to operate independently for sustained periods of time. When deploying into the deep bush for a fortnight or so, it translated into carrying a lot of weight. Whilst water could often be drawn from natural sources, for a variety of reasons this could not be relied upon. Therefore drinking water had also to be carried in sufficient quantity to sustain the soldier within the hot environs of the bush. As well as personal equipment, some items would also be carried. A spare radio battery and a belt of dislink or a 100 round drum for the RPD, dependent upon which weapon the machine gunner was using.

When preparing equipment, it was frightening to realise that the weights carried could often exceed the bodyweight of the man carrying it. Under normal circumstances lugging such loads across difficult terrain for days on end would be demanding, but to do so whilst moving tactically, with the ever present threat of ambush at every turn meant that recce operations were definitely not for the faint hearted.

It was my chance to become involved in a reconnaissance mission and I must admit to being excited. This type of work was of particular interest to me and I was eager to get started. My Stick was tasked to carry out a ten day long patrol along the Rhodesian side of the border with Mozambique.

Over the past months the area had become a focus of activity for ZANLA infiltration. Our mission was simple, handrail the border and be on the lookout for signs of terrorist movement. Follow any fresh spoor leading into Rhodesia then locate and identify whoever was responsible for making the trail.

Myself not included, my Stick comprised blokes by the names of Dave, Terry and Chris. Chris, a full Corporal, was the callsign commander. Dave was our radio operator and Terry, a talented tracker, was the man responsible for interpreting any spoor. A good tracker such as Terry could read spoor as if they were reading a book. He could tell how many men had created a trail, how long ago they had made the tracks. Yes, a good tracker was an invaluable asset. Together we were a tight team, the others having quickly accepted me into the fold.

We boarded an Alouette and were choppered out to our start point. As the Alouette landed we were out and into all round defence while the heli lifted off and clattered away.

After the noise subsided we were left alone with nothing but each other and the sounds of the African bush. Hauling on our backpacks, we set out. We patrolled northwards through close country. The heat was stifling and the air bone dry. I had soon broken out in a terrific sweat which quickly permeated my uniform to the extent it was sticking to me.

We patrolled for the remainder of the day, on a couple of occasions coming within 500 metres of the Mozambique border. We couldn't hunt for spoor at night so our operations were confined to daylight hours. As soon as the sun went down we turned over to another routine. We would find a suitable place to base up for the night before it got dark. Somewhere which afforded cover from view, but whilst allowing us to see out was ideal, yet more often than not we were forced to compromise. Our own cover was always the over-riding priority, especially here in the centre of live terrorist infiltration routes. We showed no lights and the smokers never smoked. We also never cooked food, relying instead on cold rations for the duration of the operation. The reason for the former was obvious. Shining lights, even lights from a lit cigarette could be observed by anyone in the vicinity. Smoking and cooking generated smells. Smells carried on the breeze could be easily picked up by predators or keen nosed enemies. It may seem fanciful, but for that same reason we never used scented soap or deodorants of any kind. The very last thing we wanted to do was alert anyone or anything to our presence. While there were four of us, there could be a hundred terrorists skulking through the bush close by.

Aside from routine personal admin, eating etc, we all had to take our turn on sentry duty. 'Stag' was another vital component in the security of our group. Here in hostile territory, you could just go off to sleep and hope for the best, at all times one man would be on stag, watching and listening for signs of movement.

The night passed quickly. I did my two turns on stag and spent the rest of the time sleeping fitfully. Because of the heat and the tactical situation, we only had mats and a blanket; no sleeping bags. We could get out from under the blanket a darn sight quicker than trying to kick our way out of a sleeping bag. Because of the possibility of compromise, we also slept with our boots on.

As dawn broke the following morning Dave had already put in a scheduled radio sitrep and we were prepared for the off. We resumed the patrol, moving steadily on the same bearing as the previous day.

We had been patrolling all morning, taking a five minute break each hour to rest and do map appreciations and navigation checks. We had been moving along a low rise, careful not to skyline ourselves, and were within sight of the border when we saw a Mozambique police Landcruiser bumping slowly through the bush towards us. We immediately went to ground. The Landcruiser stopped before crossing into Rhodesian territory and four uniformed police got out. One of them had a pair of binoculars and spent a good five minutes scanning our side of the border. The others then each had a turn with the glasses. They were unaware that they themselves were under observation. We wondered what on earth they were up to. They weren't looking for escaped convicts, not here in the depths of the bush. Were they scouting for a FRELIMO or ZANLA raiding party? Did FRELIMO use the civilian police for such things? Were they real police or FRELIMO disguised as police? It was perplexing.

The policemen spent about half an hour talking amongst themselves and pointing in our general direction (though there was no way they could have seen us or known of our presence) before climbing aboard the Landcruiser and heading back to where they came from.

Chris thought it a conundrum worth reporting so had Dave sent an unscheduled report over the big means patrol radio. We were told to stay put and await further orders. In due course HQ came on the net and told us to hold our position until the next day. They must have thought the same as us that the police/FRELIMO in disguise was possibly scouting for a crossing point.

We set up a covert OP on the face of the ridge where we could see along the border in either direction for quite some way. If Freddie or ZANLA wanted to come this way then they wouldn't go unseen….

We spent the rest of the day and the following night waiting. If the terrorists crossed they would most likely do so under cover of darkness. They weren't as well disposed as us when it came to ensuring that they made no noise when they moved. As soon as we either heard or saw them, Dave would call in on the special open frequency. Come daybreak we would move to intercept their tracks and the task of hunting them down would begin in earnest.

Our wait passed without incident. It was midday before we finally moved off to resume our patrol. Before we did, we backtracked several hundred metres just to satisfy ourselves that the terrorists hadn't indeed crossed without our knowledge.

We had been on patrol for five days and in all that time we hadn't seen as much as a solitary footprint. If the enemy was about then he was certainly making a good job of evading us!

That night we made camp on a small flat topped kopje which offered an excellent all round view. I had done my first stint on stag and was trying to get some sleep when I felt Dave's hand on my shoulder. He had already alerted Terry and Chris and beckoned me to join them. He pointed out a feeble light in the distance. It was difficult to tell exactly how far away it was but it kept flashing on and off in a very unusual pattern. Being a radio man, Dave knew it wasn't Morse code. We all took turns to watch through the binoculars but still couldn't make head nor tale of it. It appeared that someone out there was attempting to signal someone else but was using a system which was unknown to us. There were no points of habitation in the vicinity, so it wasn't likely to be innocent locals (why would they be out here signalling anyway?) It could possibly be poachers. Any RSF units wouldn't show lights – there were no friendly units here – we would have been informed had that been the case so as to avoid a potential blue on blue contact. Yes, poachers seemed a fair bet, either that or ZANLA.

It was my turn to look through the binos when the penny finally dropped. I suddenly realised that it wasn't someone flashing a light. It was in fact a camp fire and the reason it appeared to be sporadically flashing was that someone was moving around it, putting them self between us and it and giving the impression that it was some sort of signal lamp!

A contact at last? Chris decided to send Terry and I forward to conduct a close in recce. We had to be sure what we were seeing out there were enemies and not some innocents or poachers. For this mission, we were carrying Soviet issue weapons. I had been lugging an RPD around since our deployment. It was lighter than the standard MAG and thus easier to carry for recce work, but it was no good for this job so Chris swapped it for his AK47. Usually we used FN rifles but the AK could be fired on full auto with reasonable accuracy. In contrast the FN, while fully auto capable, was uncontrollable if used that way. Having the ability to shoot our rifles on automatic increased the weight of fire we could bring down if we found ourselves in a contact.

Our job was to find the exact location of the camp in relation to our own position and ascertain the identity, strength and dispositions of those within it. We moved up slowly, exercising caution all the way, until we were within fifty metres of the camp. There was plenty of cover but we had to be careful not to be seen or trip any hidden devices. The terrs never used AP mines or trip flares to defend their encampments but it was always better to be safe than sorry.

The fire they had burning, although small, was bright enough to allow us an overview of the situation. They were terrorists alright; the assault rifles confirmed the fact. They appeared relaxed and we caught their conversation and the occasional laugh. They were based up in a little bit of dead ground which afforded them cover enough for their needs.

Indeed, had not been for the fact that we were on high ground, it's doubtful we would have spotted them.

There were about fifteen of them in all, some were mooching about the fire while others sprawled untidy about under blankets trying to sleep. A couple of them were on stag but they looked disinterested in their duties and were simply sat on the fringes of the camp looking in at what was happening round the fire.

We spent about half an hour watching them from the safety of the shadows before retracing our steps back to our own position. We gauged the distance between them and us at about 600 metres. They were west of our location and approximately three Ks from the border. That last fact meant that they would be able to disappear quickly across into Mozambique as soon as they heard the approach of a Fireforce mission. Fortunately for us, our current position meant we were ideally placed to interdict them. We were a little far away perhaps, but our commanding view of the area negated that point. We had no idea if they were inward or outward bound.

Chris had compiled a short message which was encrypted into shackle code by Dave then transmitted back to base.

Sometime later we received our orders. A Fireforce was going to be launched against the terrorist camp at dawn. We were to act as stop group. Three Sticks of troops would arrive to the west of the target and sweep forwards, shooting it out with the enemy and driving the rest onto our position.

There was still time for us to get some sleep and we did, though I don't really think I managed to drop off fully. I was too hyped up from my close encounter during the sneaky peek and the prospect of the action to come. A good half hour before the Fireforce was scheduled to begin we were already in position. The RPD was back in my possession and had been handed a couple of spare 100 rounds drums which Chris and Terry were carrying.

In that slack period between darkness and daylight, the early sounds of wildlife drifted through the bush. We could see no sign of movement from the direction of the enemy camp but fools that they were, the terrorists had left their camp fire smouldering all night. A thin wisp of smoke rose from the trees to mark their exact location for us.

We had a good position here. The ground twixt us and the terrs was fairly open, with just a scattering of trees and thorn bushes dotted here and there. We could see over one hundred metres to our front and sides. When ZANLA came we would have plenty of warning. We had to let them get close though, fifty metres or less would be ideal, that way we increased our chances of killing them. Just in case they wanted to attack us, we had placed a couple of command detonated claymore mines at the base of the slope. Chris could initiate these mines individually should the terrs get too close. If exploded the claymore would throw out a cluster of ball bearings in an arc which would kill or incapacitate anyone caught in it.

For the fourth time I checked my weapon then took a long pull of warm water from my canteen. I had refilled it from a local water source and was forced to treat it with a purification tablet. As a result it tasted of chlorine. It was truly awful. But now, only ten minutes later, my mouth was dry again. I couldn't drink now, not until it was all over because I couldn't risk taking my eyes off the killing zone.

Before long we heard the faint thud of the approaching helicopters. The thwack of rotor blades grew rapidly louder. We were sure the terrs would have heard the noise too and were scrambling from their blankets in panic.

The three G cars came in low and fast. They disappeared briefly as they dropped the troops then whirled away, skirting wide to avoid ground fire and taking up positions in a lazy circuit behind us where the door gunners hoped to interdict any fleeing gooks. The pop and rattle of small arms fire rent the air. Momentarily the shooting was heavy but it seemed to tail off as quickly as it started. This could only mean one thing, the terrorists were running. Hopefully they were running in our direction….

Even though I was expecting them, the sight of the terrs sprinting from the bush made me jump. There were six or seven of them, running in a loose group. We held our fire and let them come on. When they were about thirty metres away Chris gave the order. We opened up. They had no chance. I kept my finger on the trigger and simply hosed them down. The RPD and three AKs concentrated a terrific volume of fire into such a small space. The ground literally erupted among the enemy as I fired a fifty round burst! Green tracer from my RPD was hitting the earth and bouncing away in wild tangents towards the trees. Amazingly, some of the gooks weren't hit and they scattered to all points whilst being harried by my RPD.

It was all over for us in less than a minute. I was now well into my second drum. Apart from the occasional gunshot fired from places we couldn't see at targets we also couldn't see, silence fell across the area. That silence was soon punctuated by the occasional burst of machinegun fire as the Alouette tech guys' spotted human movement in the bush.

We were in radio contact with the ground units now and were ordered to cease fire while they conducted their sweep.

After the area had been cleared and secured, we left our positions to meet up with the troops. It had been a good operation. The headcount was eight terrorists dead, and five wounded and or captured. Our success was not lost on us. At a stroke we had managed to eliminate all but a couple of men from a ZANLA gang. As for the surviving two, they may well have been wounded, they could even have suffered fatal wounds, but we would never know. If they managed to make it home, they would have a story to tell which would send shivers down the spines of the terrorists who were due to cross the border.

Before the others flew back to base we were replenished with food and water and took some ammo recovered from the gook camp. Once the assault team left the scene we recommenced our patrol.

The rest of the patrol was uneventful. When it ended we were removed by helicopter back to Hot Springs. We were tired, smelly, dirty and unshaven. No sooner had we made it into camp than we were ambushed by a Staff Sergeant who bellowed at us to 'get effing cleaned up!' It was wonderful to be home....!

***

From then on I knew I had found my vocation within the army. I absolutely loved recce work.

We had a few days leave. Chris and Terry went home to see their wives, leaving Dave and myself to hitch a lift into Hot Springs for a two day jolly. Hot Springs had been a popular tourist resort before the bush war had encroached upon it. Now it was a front line town, with a curfew and an oppressive feeling of constant unspoken tension among the population. In hindsight, it was not the best of choices to spend our leave, but seeing as both Dave and I had no family to speak of, we thought it as good as anywhere. We toured the bars and became known in them all. We even got to sleep in one of them after the owner took pity on us when we were running low on cash.

***

Soon after we returned to duty, ZIPRA terrorists shot down a Rhodesia Airways civilian passenger plane. The scum responsible had used a Soviet supplied Strela shoulder launched surface to air missile. They had done the same to another airliner not long before. On that occasion there had been survivors, but the terrs moved in and butchered them all. This time all the people aboard were killed in the crash.

As far as I'm aware, those responsible managed to escape back to Zambia. There was no condemnation from the international community. To them acts of barbarism such as this was entirely acceptable, just so long as they were perpetrated against Rhodesians.

We had been back on duty for a few weeks; in that time there was a spike in ZANLA activity. It was a usual ZANLA and ZIPRA tactic to place landmines on our communications network in order to disrupt movement by vehicle and kill civilians. Most of the roads were 'strip' roads, two ribbons of tarmac laid along a dirt road. It was quite easy to place mines on the miles of deserted highways and the tactic was often profitable for the terrs. They could tie up precious military resources and disrupt traffic. Sometimes the braver terrorists would place command detonated devices and lay in wait for an unsuspecting car to pass by. On rare occasions they may even wait for a military convoy, detonating an anti-tank mine under the leading vehicle before attacking the rest with small arms and RPG rockets.

As a counter to this problem, vehicles moved in convoys protected by the military. I mentioned earlier about farmers placing homemade armoured turrets on the backs of trucks, well they also used these vehicles when in convoys. Apart from the troops assigned to defend them, all the people travelling in these convoys were heavily armed. They had all manner of assault rifles, SMGs and LMGs with which to strike back in the event of a terrorist ambush. Many of the males had previous military experience, or were serving with the reserve units, so they knew how to use their weaponry to its best advantage. Little wonder that the terrs – cowards that they were – preferred to seed roads with mines then leave the scene before they got shot up.

As a further counter to the threat of mines, the Rhodesians had come up with an assortment of indigenously designed and manufactured military vehicles. All based on existing light or commercial chassis and running gear, the Crocodile, Hippo and others were a leap forward in mine protection. I believe they were the first to incorporate V type hulls to disperse the force of mine blasts. They had other neat touches too like water filled tyres, these helped to deaden an explosion. Wings and wheels were designed to blow off and direct any energy out and away from the vehicle. Then there was the 'Pookie', a strange looking moon buggy type contraption with an armoured cab. The Pookie had extremely wide tyres to lessen the pressure it placed on the road – it could run over an AT mine without detonating it. The Pookie also boasted an array of mine detectors. Where it was employed, it was always at the head of a convoy, where it could warn of any hidden mines.

***

We were kept busy at Hot Springs but I had not gotten into any more contacts. ZANLA were proving unusually elusive. On several occasions they slipped out of our Fireforce nets before we could get to grips with them.

My Stick was assigned another recce patrol. We were to deploy for ten days, again hand railing the Rhodesian/Mozambique border in the hope of picking up signs of terrorist incursion. On this occasion though, there was to be an unusual addition to our team. A tracker from the TF was to accompany us. This put Terry's nose out of joint a bit until we were told that the bloke in question was an expert in the field. It was hoped that he might be able to pick up and follow spoor which may otherwise be missed. Like Chris, he was a full Corporal; however it was made clear that Chris was callsign commander. He was quite a bit older than us, I'd say early thirties, and he was doing his call up. His name was Brian and upon meeting him we all agreed he was a solid ouen.

We spent the day prepping and the following morning was moved by truck to the start point. It wasn't lost on any of us that, should we get into trouble, a single Alouette would not be able to lift us to safety. At a pinch we could abandon our kit in order to squeeze an extra passenger aboard, but the likelihood of the RhAF endangering one of their precious machines by overloading it remained remote. We would just have to make sure we didn't find ourselves in the shit….

For three days we patrolled parallel to the border. We toiled long and hard for many hours across rough terrain under the blazing African sun.

Early on the fourth day Brian picked up spoor. In all honesty none of us would have seen it, not even Terry. Brian estimated there to be about forty terrorists, and they had passed this way less than twenty four hours ago. Chris got Dave to call the discovery in on the radio. By way of reply we were ordered to follow the trail up.

We would now track the terrorists down until we discovered their location. Then, as usual, a Fireforce mission would be mounted. Although the terrs were a day ahead, our prospects of finding them were good as they tended not to cover much distance during a day's march.

We were also aware that they may have left a surprise in their wake to be found by any Rhodesian troops. Concealed booby traps or ambush were an ever present threat. We would have to move quickly, yet we would have to be methodical and remain absolutely alert at all times.

Even though I had the RPD, I was point man, with Terry, Chris then Dave following on behind. In front of me was Brian. While Brian was concentrating on reading the spoor, he could also be relied upon to spot any hidden EDs at the same time. It was my job was to watch the front for possible ambush points and signs of enemy activity.

We were moving through close country and had cut our spacing so we could see one another. We had been following up the spoor for several hours and were all knackered from the strain of continuous hard concentration. Over time the terrain opened up into a mixture of open ground and scattered trees. We stopped at the edge of one of these clearings so I could assess the potential for ambush. Brian pointed out that the spoor was cutting across the clearing to the next clump of trees some thirty metres away. We couldn't box round the obstacle because there were no points of cover to either side. We would have to cross the open ground. It was a potential ambush point and as such I scanned it with the binos until I had satisfied myself that all was clear.

Brian stepped out from the cover of the scrub and I followed him. I had gone perhaps five paces when all hell broke loose. It is difficult for anyone who hasn't been in such a situation to understand how they play out on a purely personal level, so will do my best to explain how my emotions and instincts kicked in. Suddenly, and as soon as I heard the volley of shots, everything seemed to slow to a crawl. My mind was whirring at 10,000rpm but every second seemed like ten. I remember panicking and thinking to myself 'How can this be happening?' I had gone over the ground with a fine toothed comb and there was definitely no-one there! Rifle fire was flying all around me but I had yet to get hit. I saw Brian stumble and fall. He'd been shot. I thought 'This is it! I'm going to die!' As soon as I thought that I suddenly became calm and strangely accepting of my fate. I knew I was about to be killed so I wanted it to be clean. I didn't want to die a lingering, horribly painful death. In the hope of getting my way, I began to run at the small clump of rocks from behind which was emanating muzzle flashes. I was as calm as anything, just waiting for the bullet which would turn off my lights. I ran and kept running until all of a sudden I found myself at the other side of the clearing and into the clump of rocks! I couldn't understand how I'd got there! I was totally dumbstruck for what seemed like an age (but will in fact have been less than a second) before wheeling to face whoever had been shooting from behind the rocks. To my complete amazement, there, staring up at me with wide eyes were two gooks. They had both dropped their weapons and had their hands up! They had surrendered to me!

Gaining some semblance of composure, I covered them with my RPD. I then noticed that there was still a lot of fire coming from further along the tree line. They were close, within grenade range. I pulled a frag out of my chest webbing and pulled the pin; lobbing it high onto the spot I thought the enemy was located. It exploded and must have put the wind up them because they simply upped and ran away. It helped them along with a couple of fired from the hip bursts from my RPD but didn't hit anyone.

After the contact had ended the others caught up with me. They couldn't believe what I'd done. I couldn't believe it either. While Terry was helping to secure the ambush site, he came across another terrorist. He had been caught full on by my grenade and was taking his last breaths. Chris ordered Dave to get on the big means and call in a chopper to take our prisoners and casevac Brian. Brian had been hit in the wrist and it looked like a bad wound. The bone was shattered and he was in much pain. We gave him first aid and morphine, marking him so that the medics back at base knew he had been administered the drug.

We were told to move to a location 2ks south of the contact point from where an Alouette could get in to do the extraction. Before we set off I all but collapsed. I was suffering from exactly the same symptoms as when I had seen my friend die. Chris and the others thought I was suffering from dehydration and forced water and salt tablets down my throat. It took at least five minutes for me to recover (much quicker than had I been really suffering from dehydration). I didn't say anything, but I knew it was the delayed shock thing again.

I have thought about that incident on many occasions. I honestly think that had I turned to get under cover, or even moved one step to either side, I would have been hit. I was helped by the fact that under interrogation, the two gooks I captured admitted to being on their first mission into Rhodesia. When they saw this 'crazy' soldier charging at them, they simply panicked and gave up the fight. All I can say is it was a miracle I wasn't shot dead.

We arrived at the LZ and called the chopper in. Afterwards we made our way back to the ambush site. We were going to pick up where we left off because we were sure that the main body of terrs were not close enough to hear the exchange of gunfire or see the helicopter. The stay behind group would have been ordered to head back for Mozambique after getting into a contact. There was no way they main party would want the splinter group to join them because, in their haste to escape the scene, they were sure to leave spoor which a blind man could follow.

Terry picked up the trail and we set off after the main terrorist gang once more. Laying up that night, we whispered about my insane 'charge of the Light Brigade' moment. I never told them the real reason why I did what I did. I just allowed them to think I was a 'crazy bastard'.

The next day we set out to close on the terrorists. We were confident that, barring any more hitches, we should catch up with them by nightfall. They would be off guard because they expected their ambush team to deal with any Rhodesian follow up. To his credit Terry kept on the spoor and it led us across some exceptionally rough terrain. The terrs seemed to be moving roughly south west all the time, with very little deviation. On occasion Terry lost the spoor and we wasted time while he picked it up again. Eventually, towards the day's end the spoor had completely petered out. We were in open country now and try as he might; Terry was unable to regain the trail. It was just one of those things. Perhaps Brian the expert may have had better luck, but we would never know. If we were to take one thing away from this, it was the fact that ZANLA were beginning to take serious precautions to stop us from following them up. It wasn't only that we had been ambushed, but that they had been careful enough whilst moving across country to leave little sign of their passing.

The patrol ended without further incident. News of what happened during the ambush preceded us. According to the story, I had made some kind of heroic charge against a prepared enemy position whilst under heavy fire and single handedly broken up the enemy action without regard for my personal safety. I suppose it was true in a way but, like I said, that wasn't my intention, in fact quite the opposite. I never corrected anyone because I feared they may see me as a liability.

Later on word came that I was to be recommended for a gallantry award. I ended up with a 'Commanders Commendation'.

***

By March I had been with the RLI for four months. During that time we had lost three men killed and several more who were permanently incapacitated as a result of the gunshot wounds they sustained. There were others who had been less seriously wounded and were away from active duty while their bodies healed. It was a high stakes game of chance. None of us knew who would be next. We all thought it could never happen to us, but the truth was that it probably would….

I was promoted to Lance Corporal. Given the length of my tenure with the Battalion, there must have been some negative reaction to this in certain quarters. After all, there were plenty of men who had served far longer than me and had more practical experience of soldiering. However, the fact was that when I began basic training at Llewellyn barracks, I had been recommended for officer selection. I declined to walk that particular path but, when it was offered to me, I elected to join the NCO training course instead. It may seem strange to ex soldiers from other armies, but the Rhodesian army ran training courses for recruits who they deemed suitable for rapid promotion. If successful, said recruits could pass out as junior NCOs, even Sergeants, before joining their respective units. I successfully completed the course and was all set to join the Intelligence Corps as a full Corporal when fate overtook me.

Upon my arrival at Llewellyn I volunteered for the RLI. The paperwork had been done yet some administrative cock up had seen my application mislaid. Within the limits of what I was able to do as a recruit and latterly NCO candidate, I had kept asking about my transfer. Nothing came of it until the eleventh hour, when I was released before formally joining Int Corps and allowed to travel to Cranborne, the RLI depot in Salisbury, to begin Commando training. The price I paid for the army's blunder was that I had to relinquish my freshly sewn on stripes. It was a small price to pay for a big opportunity. All was not in vain, as I was convinced that the NCO course (which centred on infantry skills and management at sub unit levels) would stand me in good stead further down the line. The RLI were obviously aware of this as the details were contained within my records. I can only presume they thought it prudent to use someone who had undergone what they knew to be an intensive and comprehensive training course and whose performance on that course was recorded as being above average.

While I remained in the Lieutenant Bentley's Troop, I was put in charge of my own Stick. I was taking the place of the previous NCO who had been seriously wounded in a Fireforce operation. The three men I was now in charge of were called Richard, Stu and Frank. They were good blokes and I already knew them and it wasn't long before I was given the opportunity to judge how they performed in combat….

A large group of ZANLA terrs had been discovered holed up in the hills to the north of our Base. In order to take them on the entire Troop was going to go into action. My new Stick was to act as reserve for the assault team. We were told that two K cars would join in to provide close air support for our attack. Again, and because of the shortage of transport helicopters, we were to arrive on scene by parachute. After a briefing we boarded the ParaDak and were away.

We reached the target, made the jump then deployed. The assault group moved forward in extended line with us close behind. It wasn't long before the shooting started. The terrs had dug themselves in to the forward slopes of a ravine. The place was boulder strewn, affording them lots of good hard cover. They felt safe, even from the attentions of the K cars, and were putting a heavy volume of fire down against us. A K car came in quite low over our location and put several bursts of cannon fire into the enemy positions. It attracted some rifle fire for its trouble and pulled away to hold where it was out of range.

Soon after the battle had been joined, one of the Stick commanders was hit and mortally wounded. My stick was still at the rear and Lieutenant Bentley ordered us forward to join the main assault group. In a brief shouted issue of instructions, Bentley told me I was to take the wounded mans place then make an assault on the terrorists left flank. The weight of fire being brought down on us by the gooks was tremendous and it had effectively brought our advance to a standstill. There were rounds impacting all over the place, whining off rocks and hitting the dirt. Green tracers (the gooks weapons used green tracer rounds) were searching us out at every turn. Such was the volume of fire that, as I went forwards, I had to crawl the final few metres to reach the wounded Corporals Stick.

We were now amongst the rocks at the base of a steep incline and the nearest terrs were no more than twenty metres away. They had AK47s on automatic and were firing long haphazard bursts into our position. I couldn't really assess the situation without sticking my head out from cover which, given the amount of incoming, was not a sensible idea. Knowing that Bentley wanted the terrs flank turned, I sent Stu and Frank up beyond the end of their line with orders to dislodge them with grenades. While Stu and Frank made their move the rest of us would provide covering fire.

There was plenty of cover but Stu and Frank didn't get far. As soon as the terrs spotted them and opened fire they backed off. It was immediately obvious that they had gone as far as they were willing to go. We were now stalled, as was the rest of the Troop. I told the blokes to keep up their fire and motioned Richard to follow me. We scrambled and slithered, under fire all the way, to where the Stu and Frank had taken shelter. I relieved them of their frags and ordered them to commence firing against the farthest most left (our left) gook positions. Regardless of return fire, they were to keep shooting until I told them to stop.

Richard and I set out to get onto the flank. There was plenty of good cover between us and the terrs (a point which I silently noted in respect to Stu and Frank aborted attempt) and, just as long as we didn't make it obvious, we would be able to close enough to use the grenades. We were on our bellies sliding like shakes through the boulders. In the heat of the firefight, and as a result of some good suppressive fire, the gooks failed to see us.

Before long we found ourselves well within grenade throwing range. Richard was close behind me and I gave him the nod. We lobbed a couple of frags in amongst the rocks where the gooks were taking shelter. They exploded with two dull thuds and I heard screaming. Getting myself onto my haunches and tight against a rock for cover, I could now use my rifle. I followed up my initial attack with another grenade. This too exploded more or less where I wanted. Suddenly a couple of terrs appeared, they were on all fours and scrambling crazily for the ridgeline. They were shot down before I could engage them. Using my remaining two grenades now, I threw them a little further into where I believed more gooks were sheltering. As soon as they went off I motioned for the boys at the foot of the slope to begin their assault. Richard and myself put down enfilade fire as the others made their move. I for one couldn't see any targets but was shooting simply to make the enemy keep their heads down.

Quite rapidly, the others advanced and found themselves among the terrorist position. The gooks had scarpered, perhaps as a result of being shot at from below or perhaps as a result of suddenly being attacked by fragmentation grenades. They had left two men dead and another dying from a chest wound.

We pushed on to the ridge then went firm as I contacted the Lieutenant on the handheld. We were occupying the high ground and overlooked the other enemy positions. Bentley told me to provide supporting fire for the other Sticks and we quickly obliged. The terrorists didn't like to be shot at from two sides so quickly began to fall back in some disorder. We killed another two of them as they ran for the ridgeline. As soon as they made the ridge they scattered and fled. In his haste to escape, one of the terrs took the wrong turn, running our way where he was promptly shot dead.

The other Sticks were now ascending the slope and the sudden noise of gunfire told us that some of the gooks had run into the stop group. A lone K car was prowling, firing its cannon at targets we could no longer see.

The shooting soon petered to nothing and we set about the task of securing the area. We had accounted for no less than ten terrorists killed along with four wounded and captured. We had also taken three other prisoners, one of whom turned out to be a FRELIMO officer. It was an exceptional result, but one for which the terrorists extracted a heavy price. We lost one man killed and another seriously wounded. The K car which was operating above us as we made our initial advance had been damaged by rifle fire and forced to withdraw.

When we got back to base I pulled Stu and Frank to one side and warned them that, in my opinion, their performance hadn't been good enough. Richard and I had managed to get up the slope from where we were able to attack the terrs with grenades and there was no reason why they couldn't have done the same. Both were adamant that they had been pinned down and were unable to advance. I didn't believe them, but because I had no proof, I left it at that….

***

The terrorists were getting bolder by the day and ranging ever deeper into Rhodesia from their bases in Zambia and Mozambique. Over a relatively short period of time ZANLA had de-railed a freight train running from South Africa to Salisbury, causing a lot of disruption to important rail traffic. They had also attacked a main fuel storage depot on the outskirts of Salisbury. Roads were being mined in areas which, until then, had been deemed relatively safe, while attacks upon farms and other remote outposts were on the increase. While the terrorists armies of Mugabe and Nkomo had a seemingly inexhaustible supply of recruits and materiel support from China and Russia respectively, the Rhodesian security forces were stretched almost beyond breaking point. Despite our best efforts, our lack of resources was taking a serious toll on our ability to defend our country against the terrorists.

In an effort to somehow redress the imbalance over on the 'eastern front'; the border between Mozambique and Rhodesia, a new tactic was being trialled. To supplement the existing stratagem of tracking terrorist groups who were already inside Rhodesia, it had been argued that it may be worthwhile to insert recce callsigns over the border into Moz to try and intercept signs of terrorist movement. This could be achieved by the use of patrols operating under the same procedures as 'internal' recce units, whereby the callsign would move parallel to the frontier in the hope of intercepting spoor, or to set up a firm base on a suitable piece of high ground within the most active areas and then be on the lookout for terrorist columns as they headed for the border. Whatever the circumstances, should movement be uncovered we would send a radio report giving time, location, numbers, heading etc. The brains back at HQ would collate this information and translate it into an accurate approximation of where and when the enemy were due to enter Rhodesian territory. An ambush party could then be organised to 'welcome' the terrs. Another useful sideline would be our ability to gather general intelligence relating to our area of operations. For example we may come across hitherto unknown FRELIMO or ZANLA positions, if so, we could mark these on our maps and upon our return they would be added to the intelligence jigsaw.

If any targets of opportunity presented themselves to us, should the RhAF have aircraft available and thought it was warranted, we were also able to direct airstrikes. It was all good proactive stuff and I was itching to be included….

My Troop had been selected to fill this new role for Three Commando and we underwent specialist training to prepare for it. It wasn't long before we were given the opportunity to try out our new skills. My Stick was tasked to carry out a mission into Moz to see what we could find. I must admit to having my reservations about Stu and Frank, but they were both experienced Troopers with some specialist skills which may prove useful.

The mission was scheduled to last seven days. The area in which we were to operate was a known hotspot of both ZANLA and FRELIMO activity. The former used it as a jumping off point for Rhodesia bound terrorists while Freddie mounted regular foot and vehicle patrols. It was a hostile environment in every respect. We were to be inserted some 30ks inside the border and had little prospect of support should things turn ugly. If we did find ourselves compromised and unable to be airlifted to safety, our only option would be to get out on foot. Thirty kilometres may not seem all that far, but if you have kicked over a hornet's nest and hundreds of angry ZANLA and Freddie's spill out to attack you, then thirty kilometres is one hell of a long way.

We were inserted by Alouette in the early hours of the morning. In order to confuse any ground units or watching FRELIMO radar operators, the G car changed course several times, the pilot flying as low as the conditions allowed.

We were very heavily laden with all the equipment and supplies required to sustain us for over a week (we took more than we needed just in case the RhAF were unable to extract us on the appointed day). We landed about ten kilometres north of our final destination, a low lying kopje which, the briefing officer assured us, would afford good views across the area.

We reached the OP without incident and settled ourselves in. The routine was to be three hours on and three hours off in rotation through each twenty four hour period. Frank and I would do one shift while Richard and Stu ate and/or slept. I had chosen Frank to be my watch buddy as I wanted to split him and Stu up. It also gave me the opportunity to observe him at work at close quarter.

The area we had under observation was quite open, thus it was relatively easy to spot movement by groups of men on foot. We had some good binoculars and, for night time work, a night vision scope. It was the first time any of us had seen such a device as they were on the sanctions list. Looking through the thing produced a green image and it was effective for several hundred metres.

Despite the area being a supposed well used area of infiltration, we saw absolutely nothing. There was a dirt road running roughly NE to SW about 500 metres from our OP and even that was utterly devoid of traffic. A few civilian vehicles traversed it, but only in daylight.

ZANLA had either slipped by without being seen (unlikely) or they were using another route.

We moved off on day seven and were airlifted home.

For the time being we were returned to Fireforce duties. I went off on another recce course and returned to find the guys as busy as ever….

***

Lieutenant Bentley called Chris and me to the Troop office. He informed us that he had been ordered to assemble a seven man recce team to be deployed across the Moz border on an extended patrol. Chris (who was a full Corporal) was to be patrol commander while I was to act as 2IC. We could choose the remaining men ourselves. It was agreed from the off that Terry, Dave and my replacement in Chris' Stick – a bloke named Pete – would go. From my own Stick I put the case forward for Richard and Stu. Richard was a good soldier, steady under fire, while Stu was a qualified radio man. We would need two radio operators on this job so Chris approved. We ran our selection past Bentley who gave his blessing then we gathered everyone together for the patrol briefing.

Although Chris and I had already been given a bare bones rundown of the mission, this was the first time we were to hear any real detail.

We were to deploy by parachute into Mozambique. We would then establish a firm base from which we could operate. From there we would work in teams of four and three with Chris or me in charge of each sub-section. While the four man team would stay behind with the supplies and a big means radio, the other would move forwards some eight kilometres and set up a covert OP on the slopes of a 400 metre high kopje which overlooked a network of dirt roads running from the interior of Mozambique towards the Rhodesian border. It was suspected that these roads were being used by ZANLA to resupply and reinforce their forward units since the destruction of the nearest bridge over the Zambezi (Funnily enough, the same operation in which we participated on Christmas Day). The OP team would remain on station, so as not to create breaks in the observation, and be resupplied when required by the firm base.

Our main task was to be on the lookout for vehicular movement along any of these roads and positively identify them as belonging to ZANLA. Once (if) we saw any such movements we were to log down all the details for transmission using the small means radio back to the firm base. They would then use the long range radio to pass on the information to Rhodesia. If a particularly important target – such as a large convoy – came our way we also had the option of requesting an airstrike. However this particular procedure would be rather long winded and meant passing the detail to the firm base (our radio did not possess the necessary range to contact HQ), and they forwarding it to Rhodesia. Once the necessary permissions had been granted the target would be well beyond our visual range, leaving the RhAF to pick up then attack it using the calculations of heading and speed we had provided at our own point of contact as a datum point from which they could estimate the current location of the target. It was certainly complicated and quite possibly very ineffective.

We had no idea as to why the powers that be wanted this area watching. We had no need to know that information. I guessed it was a precursor to an intensive mine laying and/or ambush operation against the roads to further disrupt the terrorist logistics effort. If so, then as much information as possible as to how, when and by whom the roads were being used was vital in order to prepare effective measures with which to stop them.

We made our preparations and were ready to go that same night. We were parachuting for the simple fact that we had to remain self sufficient throughout the duration of the mission. Any helicopter movements may alert FRELIMO to the possibility of the presence of Rhodesian soldiers and that could easily translate into action of some kind. Everything we needed we would take and the only way to move us and a not inconsiderable amount of equipment was by paradrop.

It was after dark that the ParaDak set off. Our insertion point was some 70ks inside Mozambique and about four kilometres from the place we were to establish the firm base. We would be in deep bush country and hopefully well away from prying eyes.

The drop went as planned and we made our way to the point where we had decided to set up the firm base. My team were the observation callsign. After resting up we set off towards the hill. There was no real need for navigation as we could see our destination in the distance.

We were moving in daylight, which may seem strange, however, given the fact that we were in close country and far removed from any points of habitation and known FRELIMO activity, it was considered safe to do so.

We reached the base of the kopje without incident. The site of our proposed OP was on the far side of the hill. This presented several potential problems, the biggest of which was the fact that once settled in, we would have a massive physical obstacle between us and the team back at the firm base. This had the potential to create a break in our communications. Without going into technical matters with which I'm not fully conversant, radio transceivers are often temperamental insofar as they are subject to the vagaries of atmosphere and terrain. This may perhaps not be the case today, but it certainly was back in the seventies. For any transceiver to work at its best, line of sight between two sets is always preferred. By placing a hill between ourselves and the firm base, especially when using a low powered set like the one we carried meant there was a very real possibility that any signals could become corrupted and thus unable to be successfully transmitted or received. We could of course get round this by making sure we transmitted from the top of the kopje, making sure we had an uninterrupted path for the signals to follow, but this was ruled out during the planning phase as being an unsuitable location for the OP. We were going to base ourselves up not far from the summit so, if we found it impossible to establish radio contact, we would have that option as a contingency. Even though we had been assured there was no ZANLA or FRELIMO ground activity within the vicinity of the hill we still exercised caution and this meant making sure we couldn't be seen. For example sky lighting oneself against the crest of the hill would not be sound practice and may lead to compromise.

The incline was steeper than any of us imagined and there were sections where we were forced to scramble up on all fours. We were heavily loaded with as much rations and water as we could carry. In the end it took several hours to move up and around the hill and identify the location of our OP.

It's safe to say that we were all fatigued by our labours, yet we could not rest until we had dug ourselves in to our position. After some twiddling of knobs and creative antennae tweaking, Stu managed to establish contact with the firm base. The signal was weak, hovering around strength one, unsatisfactory in many respects but at least it was there and fairly consistent. We remained aware that a change in the weather may knock out our comms altogether. Our plan to relocate the radio if required when we needed to transmit was dealt a blow then we saw the nature of the hillside above us. In between us and the peak were several obstacles which provided a serious challenge to anyone attempting to reach the summit. Stu would just have to soldier on and try to maintain the comms link from our current position.

In front of us and across a hundred and forty degree arc, the view was astounding. We had a virtually uninterrupted view of the area over which we were to watch as far as our binoculars could see. The ground was quite open and the dirt roads easily visible. Right on the very limit of our view, shimmering in like a mirage in the heat haze, we could just make out the fringes of the closest town.

At the base of the hill an area of quite thick woodland extended about six hundred or so metres in every direction, petering out thereafter into a series of small and sporadically sited copses which thinned further still as they reached out towards the nearest dirt road.

I passed the binoculars to Richard and he commenced the first watch. Our routine from this point on would be to rotate observation duties between the three of us, three hours on and six hours off. When I had made the initial cursory sweep of the area I had seen no sign of movement along the roads so I busied myself with personal admin. Just as I was about to settle down and attempt some sleep, Richard motioned me to his side. He had noticed a track leading from the closest dirt road to the trees. I took a look through the binoculars and was immediately intrigued. At first glance the track was not all that obvious but closer inspection revealed it to have been probably made by vehicular traffic. It wound in a shallow S from the trees to the road. What the hell?

Since our arrival the wind had been gusting hard from left to right across the forward slope, when it eventually dropped Stu had taken over from Richard to do his stint. I was asleep but was woken by Richard and asked to listen. I found myself in between Stu and Richard with my gaze following Stu's pointed finger. Looking down across the canopy of trees I heard shouts. Fuck! Someone was down there amongst the trees! Who the heck were they and what were they doing here? It immediately flashed through my mind that we had been spotted as we made our way up the hill and Freddie had arrived to flush us out. Nonsense! They could have never arrived here without our seeing them! There was supposed to be no-one within half a day's march, yet here they were. It could be coincidence that whoever was making the noise were hidden under the canopy of trees, but my nose smelt a rat. It may be the case that the mysterious occupants of the woods just didn't want to be seen.

Until we could make a positive identification there was little we could do. Richard, Stu and I were all agreed that it was highly unlikely that they were civilians. The most plausible explanation was that we had stumbled upon a ZANLA holding camp. The gooks liked to disperse their units as defence against air attack; that said to post any here, in the back of beyond some 70ks from Rhodesia, seemed improbable. Perhaps the place was a satellite camp for another larger and as yet undiscovered terrorist camp?

We could speculate all day long and get no farther forward. Before any action could be taken we would have to find out just who we were dealing with.

I got Stu to send a shackled message off to the firm base explaining the situation. The reply was some time coming, probably as a result of Chris advising Rhodesia of our possible find. We were instructed to hold firm and maintain the road watch. In the meantime, if we managed to identify the inhabitants of the woods then we should pass on our findings as a matter of priority.

It un-nerved me to think that we were in such close proximity to what may prove to be a sizeable body of enemy. Although we were well hidden, our ability to withdraw quickly should the need arise was restricted.

Come nightfall we had observed very little movement of vehicular traffic along the network of dirt roads. In contrast we were able to see several points of light emanating from beneath the canopy at the foot of the kopje. The trees were in full leaf and the cover they provided thick. Subsequently there may have been more. Throughout the day when the wind had been in our favour, we had heard regular snippets of human voices. This ranged from shouts and laughter to singing.

Our neighbours were in fine voice this evening and their songs cemented our suspicion as to their identity. They were singing songs of Chimurenga, the war of 'liberation'. No civilians would sing such songs and neither would FRELIMO. The inhabitants of the woods were ZANLA. They were indeed hiding out from Rhodesian reconnaissance aircraft and they were doing it rather well. They had no need to exercise noise discipline, just make sure they couldn't be seen from the air during daylight. The only thing which could give them away was the fresh vehicle tracks running from the nearest dirt road to the trees.

We had one more scheduled radio slot and used it to tell the firm base what we had seen and heard. If the RhAF could be persuaded to mount an airstrike, we could take out a whole group of terrorists in one fell swoop.

The following day we split our obs between road watching and observing the area of trees, writing down everything we saw and reporting it all back during our radio transmissions. To his credit, and despite the difficulties of terrain, Stu managed to maintain a steady link with Chris and the others. We were expecting to be asked to provide more detailed information about the ZANLA gang but nothing was forthcoming. I guess I was being impatient, a trait not appreciated in reconnaissance work, but I felt a golden opportunity to kill terrorists was being passed by. Because of severe constraints on resources, I just had to accept the fact that HQ may not be able to give priority I had attached to our discovery.

On day four a message from Rhodesia was relayed to us via the firm base. We were to supply the co-ordinates of the suspected enemy base and provide a positive identification of whoever was in it. The planners back in Rhodesia didn't accept our hearing a few songs as proof that the area was home to a terrorist unit. If they were to expend time and effort, time and effort which could be used productively in other areas, they had to be sure that the rewards would justify the mobilisation of precious RhAF resources.

During the time we had become aware of their presence, the terrs hadn't shown themselves and were sticking rigidly to their camouflage routines. There had been no vehicles coming to or from the trees which may give us an indication as to their identity. If we wanted to provide conclusive proof, there was only one way. We would have to mount a close reconnaissance of the camp.

The three of us had a long and detailed discussion. If we were given the go ahead, we could leave our OP and move down the hill to ground level. Once on the edge of the wooded area we would hope to spot whoever was hiding out there. If we could determine that they were indeed ZANLA, and that they were present in sufficient numbers, the RhAF would put in a strike.

In the end we determined that the road watch remained our primary objective. There had been a disappointing level of activity, but nonetheless we had to maintain our observations. We needed two men to keep the obs up, that left one to go down and take a closer look at the camp. We all agreed that it could possibly turn sour very quickly so I volunteered myself for the task. As the one with the longest service, Stu was senior and so would take charge of the OP during my absence. Despite my initial misgivings, my attitude towards Stu had changed for the better. He was a steady away sort of chap, never rushed nor really ruffled. He had proved he was a good radio operator; a skill much valued in the remote African bush.

The plan was far from ideal; however the potential rewards outweighed the risk. We put the scheme to Chris back at the firm base and got his approval. I would move down to the edge of the wooded area during the hours of darkness and find a suitable position from where I could see but not be seen. Because we already knew there was no patrol activity outside the boundaries of the trees, it was a pretty safe bet that I wasn't going to bump into any gooks. I would spend the day watching for activity and anything that allowed me to determine that they were indeed ZANLA terrorists before returning to the OP the following night. One of the lights we had spotted was not far beyond the tree line and it was this area upon which I would concentrate my efforts. I would travel light, with only my webbing and rifle. I had brought along a privately purchased pair of binoculars. Although compact, they had good quality optics and 10x magnification. My decision to pack them was a fortuitous one, as they would allow me to explore further into the wooded area than it was possible with the naked eye.

I waited until well after last light before commencing my move. Richard, Stu and I had already worked out a contingency plan in the event of my compromise. Dependent upon circumstance, they were to remain at the OP and await my return. However once the pre-arranged cut off time had passed they were to assume I had been killed or captured. As a result of the relatively open area around our OP, if the terrorists were alerted, it would be difficult to move during the hours of daylight without being seen. If they thought it safe to do so, we agreed that the best course of action was to remain on station until after dark before withdrawing. As a contingency plan B, we had set up an emergency rendezvous point (ERV) in the bush on the other side of the hill where we could meet if split. Just in case I had been compromised and evaded death or capture, but couldn't get back to the OP, I would strike out for the ERV. Once again Stu and Richard's stay at the ERV would be time limited. Had I not shown up within the allocated time frame, then they were to move back to the firm base.

Darkness came quickly. About an hour after last light I left the OP and began my descent. It was slow and hard going. I couldn't rush, there was plenty of loose earth and I didn't want to send it or any small rocks tumbling down the hill to alert anyone below. I was moving tactically and working to the assumption that the area I was passing through was under observation.

Eventually I found myself at the base of the hill and amongst an area of boulders and scrub. There was cover aplenty here and I was confident that the gooks would have to step on me to realise I was there. I had a good view of the tree line but the darkness meant it looked like a solid block of shadow. My one and only point of reference was the feeble flicker of light which glowed dimly through the trees. I settled down, drank some water and ate a little cold rations then settled down to wait….

I managed a little sleep but was awake long before dawn. The wind was blowing gently into my face and I began to smell the occasional wisp of wood smoke. Soon voices – men's voices – also began to drift in the breeze.

I was in good cover here, among a cluster of rocks and scrub, about twenty metres from the tree line. The ground twixt and me was open, save for the odd spindly bush, affording me a good view across my arc and quite some distance into the trees. Although I was danger close I felt quite secure. During our observations from the hillside, we had witnessed no movement outside the trees, no one had broken cover and there was little reason to suspect they would start now. From my hide I could see but not be seen and was confident that I could hide out here for the rest of the day.

I began to see movement. Yes, there they were, milling around the camp fire. It was difficult to estimate numbers but there were least two dozen men. They were about twenty metres inside the tree line. I brought the binoculars to bear and immediately had my suspicions confirmed. They were ZANLA alright. They were dressed in a mishmash of military garb which was typical of the terrs. I could see no weapons but why would they feel the need to carry their rifles here, where they considered themselves safe?

Within the opening hour of daylight I had confirmed the presence of a terrorist gang at this location. There was no possibility of my being able to confirm the numbers involved but, based upon the fact that we had seen several camp fires from our main OP, I estimated there could be between up to two hundred terrorists hiding out here.

After watching the terrs for a while I shrank back in amongst the rocks. My intention at that point was to mount the occasional observation in an attempt to gather more intelligence. It was pointless just staying on watch all the time as, even though I was in good cover, the chances of compromise would increase. Best then to make sure I kept my head down.

In my head I was already planning what I was going to ask Stu to transmit upon my return to the main OP. A terrorist presence was confirmed. I'd estimate numbers and request an airstrike at the earliest possible opportunity. Even if the RhAF were only to commit one Canberra jet bomber to the mission it would do grievous harm to the terrs if it dropped a payload of the small anti-personnel Alpha bombs. No, it would need more than one 'plane. The area of the target was simply too large and the enemy spread out too far within it. Two or even three Canberra's dropping 225kg high explosive bombs would be the better solution.

And so my thoughts continued at tangents. The bloody RhAF would know how best to attack the target, just leave it to them. I just had to hope that they would think it worthy of their attention in the first place. Two hundred terrs? Of course they'd think it was worth bombing! I was secretly thrilled at the prospect at being partly responsible for the demise of a large group of terrorists. It may sound callous, but I had nothing but contempt for them. Had they restricted themselves to conventional warfare, and not made it their priority to attack civilians in the ghastly fashion which they adopted, I may have thought differently. As things stood I simply hated them all with a passion.

The day passed slowly. I restricted myself to remaining well under cover and only taking occasional looks out into the trees. Nothing had changed. Sometimes I could see the terrs, sometimes I couldn't. I could still hear them quite plainly though. They seemed in high spirits. Hopefully they were soon to have their morale shattered….

It was about half an hour before last light. My plan was to wait until after darkness had settled before making a slow withdrawal.

Everything had gone well. Moving tactically, I hoped to be up at the OP within a couple of hours. Richard and Stu were only 350 metres above me but the ground separating us was open. It wasn't just a case of hiking up to the top; I had to move whilst taking advantage of all available cover. This meant making a meandering ascent which would easily double the distance to be covered. As well as tactical considerations, the hill itself was possessed of terrifically steep inclines; indeed, portions of it were almost sheer. I became aware of just how challenging the slope was on my outbound journey, so was under no illusion as to the scale of the obstacle.

Just one last look at the target. I could hear snatches of conversation intermingled with the occasional burst of laughter. I'd become accustomed to that and its volume. The gooks hadn't moved much. Slowly I showed my head from the side of the rock behind which I had been sheltering. FUCK! There, just within the tree line, was a gook. He was one big bastard. He stood not far off two metres tall and was powerfully build to boot. He was wearing camouflage pattern trousers and an olive drab shirt. He had a rifle slung over his right shoulder. He was looking in my direction. He wasn't on the alert. What was he doing there? Taking a piss? In those sixty seconds – sixty seconds which in reality would have been less than one second – my heart stopped. I saw his eyes then an expression of total surprise spread quickly across his face. He had seen me! I heard a shout as he went for his rifle. Ducking back behind the rock, I began to scramble away on all fours. There was a gunshot, then several more. The gook was shooting his AK-47 into where he thought I was hiding. A shout, running, more shouts. The terrs friends would be startled and confused by the sudden gunfire. I could turn that confusion to my advantage. However, it would soon pass and they would be out to get me. Until then they may just scatter, thinking that they were under attack by the Rhodesians.

With a combination of crawling and slithering, I was now about twenty five metres from my original location. I was still in quite good cover but was aware that I could easily expose myself. It was still light. I couldn't possibly hope to make a start up the hill because as soon as I did I would be spotted and fired upon. Hoping to add to the general disorder among the enemy I decided to lob a grenade into the trees. I pulled one from my chest webbing and threw it, hoping it or I wouldn't be seen in the process. It detonated with a solid thump. I continued to move. I had to get the hell away from the immediate area before the gooks realised that this was no Fireforce.

I was moving parallel to the foot of the kopje, keeping my head down as much as possible. Up at the OP Stu and Richard would have heard the commotion and know things had gone wrong.

There was some more shooting now. I don't know where from, but it was light and sporadic. It looked like the terrs were finally coming to the conclusion that their base wasn't under attack. I suddenly realised that it had been a mistake to throw the grenade. I might have gotten away with it otherwise. The gooks would have questioned their man and done a search of the area. When they found nothing they may well just have assumed that he was mistaken. It was wishful thinking of course, but by my throwing the frag, I had confirmed what the terr told his comrades. I silently chastised myself for being so bloody stupid.

I was still moving and my direction of travel hadn't changed. At long last the light began to fade. I found a piece of good cover and went to ground. I could hear shouts and general noise of movement away to the point of contact. The gooks were beginning to organise themselves and wanted to know who was out there on the edge of their hidden encampment. If they weren't already, they'd soon begin to search the scrubland at the base of the hill and that would bring some of them in my direction. This notion prompted me to make another move. I wanted to put as much distance as possible between them and me before I began the climb.

At long last the sun set. Although I was desperate to move, I waited until it was fully dark before finally breaking cover. There were several points of activity around me now, with a couple perhaps as close as thirty metres. It was all haphazard stuff. The gooks seemed to be stumbling about without any direction. Despite the uncoordinated efforts of ZANLA, I knew that by staying where I was I was simply inviting discovery.

Taking a deep breath and doing my best to ensure I wouldn't be seen, I left the scrub and began the climb. Instead of going straight up, I went at forty five degrees. It was easier this way and, if spotted, I wouldn't be leading the terrs back to the others.

Thankfully, in the slack period between the fall of the sun and the rise of the moon, it was pitch black. I made the most of this sudden advantage, clambering up and away from the terrorists below with a much of a combination of speed and stealth as I could muster.

As predicted, it took me a good two hours to reach the OP, mostly because of the climb, the tactical nature of the move and partly because I had difficulty locating it. I made myself known to the others so that they wouldn't open up on me before gratefully scrambling into the position.

Richard and Stu had heard the shooting so knew things had gone wrong. As per our plan, they had been giving me time to return before pushing off. I explained what happened and asked Stu to get a report to the firm base. He had already been in contact with them after they became aware of the possible compromise. Stu warned me that we were on our last battery, we had brought spares but, because of the fact he had been forced to operate the radio on full power to overcome the difficulties of transmission, we had used them all. I knew we would need our small means later on so I scrubbed the idea. If we sent a message off from the other side of the hill then we would have line of sight. That being the case the transmission could be made on a low power setting, thus saving the battery.

We prepared to move. The plan was simple, we would go up and over the summit then work our way down to ground level. Once off the hill we would strike out for the firm base and link up with Chris and the others.

We collected all our kit and set off. Although I had visually inspected it upon our arrival, taking in the difficulties of any move to the summit, at that point I still hadn't fully appreciated the scale of the obstacle and thought it would be quicker to go up and over rather than work our way slowly round the hill. We soon realised that the assault on the peak was not going to be as straightforward as we presumed. What looked like a difficult yet entirely scalable obstacle from below became something entirely different when we attempted to ascend it Although it was only about fifty metres away the ground was terribly steep and we were forced to climb what amounted to a fifteen metre high rock face which separated us from it. Had we not been burdened by rifles and personal equipment then the task would indeed have been much easier but, as it stood, we really struggled.

We weren't worried about being seen at that stage. ZANLA was still running about down below and could not possibly spot us in the darkness at this altitude.

Once we crested the peak I had Stu send the message. The guys back at the firm base were maintaining a listening watch and picked it up immediately. They acknowledged then came back with a reply none of us wanted to hear.

Back in Rhodesia the signals intelligence people had been monitoring FRELIMO radio traffic stating that Freddie was being deployed into the area to hunt for Rhodesian troops. That really put the wind up us. Several hours had passed since the compromise, plenty of time for FRELIMO to receive an alert then arrive in sufficient numbers to begin a search. We had been too busy scaling the peak to bother looking down towards the trees so we hadn't seen any evidence of vehicle movements, nor had we heard anything. The wind wasn't in our favour, easily blowing the sound of vehicles in the opposite direction. We could also assume that Freddie would be running with lights out. I cursed my rash decision to throw that bloody grenade, though I didn't tell the others what I'd done.

Our priority now was to get off this damned hill. It was a given that the FRELIMO units which had been dispatched to hunt for us would deploy around the base off the hill to seal off any potential escape routes. Freddie was many things, but stupid wasn't one of them. He would quickly realise that ZANLA had most likely encountered a Rhodesian reconnaissance team. He'd work out the best place to mount any observation was from the hill. Looking at their maps they could also possibly determine the significance of the nearby road network to their ZANLA allies and establish another reason for our presence.

Descending the kopje proved every bit as arduous as the climb. There was no cover – which wasn't a real issue given the hour of the day, but the nature of the ground itself was tortuous. There were areas of loose shale which could easily send the unwary into an uncontrollable tumble and a thousand places where an ankle could be turned. Instead of taking the direct route, we were forced to zigzag, avoiding the obstacles as best as we could.

As we moved to within a hundred metres of the kopje's base I took a little time out to scan the area below with the NVG. Alerted to the FRELIMO action, we had been watching and listening for any signs of movement. Although we had neither seen nor heard anything to suggest an enemy presence, that didn't mean they weren't there. I had to assure myself that we weren't walking into an ambush.

Although exhausted from our exertions, we made to ground level in one piece. The priority now was to clear the immediate area then find a laying up point (LUP) where we could spend the rest of the day. While it had been acceptable to make our initial approach to the kopje in daylight, now that FRELIMO and (possibly) ZANLA were actively searching for us, it was dangerous to move while the sun was up. We were on the dregs of our battery, but I chanced a short transmission to inform Chris that we had made it off the hill, were striking out for an LUP and that we planned to return to the firm base during the coming night.

Although we were doing our best to anti-track, we were all aware that Freddie had some bloody good people who could pick up and interpret the minutest traces of spoor. With that in mind we set off. We weren't heading for the firm base as we didn't wasn't to lead the enemy to Chris and the others, instead we cut away on another bearing. The priority now was to find somewhere to hide….

We patrolled about two kilometres from the hill, moving tactically all the way and using the available cover to our best advantage. The sun was already up by the time we found a suitable LUP. It was a small area of dead ground covered with a scattering of brush. It was far from ideal as our ability to observe the surrounding area was severely restricted, however it provided solid cover. We slithered on our bellies beneath the low lying branches of a mature bush and settled down. Apart from a dying radio battery, we were also short of food and water. A resupply had been due from the firm base, but I had rescheduled it for the night just passed. Another mistake!

We ate a little and drank sparingly. If things continued to go wrong then it was likely we wouldn't make it back to the firm base and we'd be stuck, some seventy kilometres from home. There was no chance of any rescue. The RhAF wouldn't be able to locate us and didn't have the resources to come looking. Without any means of communication, we'd be screwed. I didn't mention this to Richard and Stu, but I was already planning our escape. Seventy kilometres to the border, that was as the crow flies. Deviating whilst evading FRELIMO may add another twenty or thirty klicks. We could do it. If we kept our cool and steered clear of any contacts, we could make Rhodesia in five or six days? Even if we severely rationed ourselves from this point on we hadn't enough food or water to sustain us more than a couple of days. With luck we could draw water from natural sources, but we'd have to go hungry. Of course there was the small matter of getting to civilisation once back home. We couldn't just go walking up to the nearest farm for fear of being mistaken for gooks and fired at. There was also the possibility of running into our own ambush teams or indeed the terrs themselves. As I lay down to attempt some sleep I tried to push such thoughts out of my mind. I did manage to drift off, but with the image of that bloody grenade floating through my head. Stupid bastard….

Stu was taking first stag and he woke Richard and me when he heard it. The voices were coming from the bush north of our location. We were unable to accurately determine distance, but estimated they were about fifty metres away. Often FRELIMO and ZANLA had little regard for noise discipline, even in circumstances such as this. So, the enemy was out here searching for us. The voices came closer then suddenly sheared off into the distance. Shortly afterwards there was more noise. Orders being issued and the clanking of unsecured kit drifted through the bush from several tens of metres away. We still couldn't see anything but it was obvious we had been overtaken and possibly encircled. In response to a question from Stu, I whispered that I didn't think the enemy knew our location. They were being far too indifferent. Had they known they would have approached cautiously, making as little noise as possible. They were looking for us alright, but didn't know where we were.

We were on the alert now. We had about twelve hours of daylight left before we could move, plenty of time for Freddie to find us….

After completing a map appreciation I had a hushed conversation with the others. Closing up so our whispering could be understood, we assessed the situation. Should we stay here and hope that Freddie might pass us by? Should we move in the hope that we could ease our way out of the encirclement and thus avoid being killed or captured? I was worried that we had not done enough to stop a determined tracker from hunting us down. If we stayed put were we only waiting for the inevitable to happen? Moving in close proximity to the enemy in daylight posed obvious and serious risks, but the closeness of the country was in our favour. Freddie was making plenty of noise and giving us warning of his whereabouts. If we moved could we avoid him? We were all agreed that the FRELIMO we heard were advance units, moved into the area quickly to try and locate us. They wouldn't have sufficient numbers to conduct a proper cordon and search operation, not yet anyway. That would change when reinforcements arrived. Our next move was put to the vote….

We crawled out of our hiding place and set off at a very slow patrol pace. We were moving northwards. We all knew where we were going and what to do in the event of a contact and our becoming split. The coordinates of the ERV was embedded in our heads.

I was on point, with Stu then Richard following up. We were moving in increments of twenty five metres, stopping to look and listen for any hint of the enemy each time before commencing the next leg. We heard nothing to suggest that Freddie was in the immediate vicinity but came across spoor which suggested a group of men, possibly fifteen strong, had crossed from left to right, cutting through our line of march.

I slowed down the pace. We were moving deliberately, hugging cover and scanning our arcs. Any paces of open ground were 'boxed'; staying within cover we moved around the edges before returning to our original course.

About an hour or so into the move we heard vehicles moving to our front and left. This was not good news. Far from breaking through the perimeter of the FRELIMO search effort, we were still firmly inside it. Vehicles only meant one thing; Freddie was bussing in more troops to join in the hunt. Hunkering down in the first available patch of good cover, Richard, Stu and I had a hurried discussion. We had only moved about 500 metres from our LUP and had no idea how much further we needed to travel before we slipped through the net. One thing in our favour appeared to be the continued disorganised nature of the FRELIMO search effort. They seemed to be cross graining the bush without any plan of action. However, disorganised or not, we could still find ourselves getting into a contact at any moment….

We continued to patrol, zigzagging our course with regular frequency to stay in cover but also throw any Freddie trackers off course. We continued to hear occasional shouts and whistle blasts, accompanied by the odd vehicle or two, yet none close enough to cause us real alarm. It was perhaps three hours since we moved off and I estimated that, as the crow flies, we had not yet covered one kilometre. With all the meandering the actual distance walked would have been nearer two.

The ground was becoming open, making it more difficult for us to move without being seen. I brought Richard and Stu to a halt with a hand signal before motioning them into the crouch. There, about seventy metres ahead, was a FRELIMO lorry. Two Freddie's were stood up in the back. It was parked side on to us and I could see it clearly with the naked eye. The two Freddie's were manning a machinegun which they had set up on its bipod on the cab roof. I took the binos and carefully scanned the truck and its surroundings. Apart from the machinegun team, a few of their mates were milling around the truck. They were all armed and seemed only vaguely alert. One or two of them were smoking while a couple more were lounging up against the tailgate. They gave the impression that they weren't expecting trouble. I motioned my intentions to the others and, very carefully, we reversed in slow time before cutting left and boxing around the obstacle.

Having successfully escaped the attentions of the FRELIMO lorry team, we swung back on course. We were still moving slowly as we all knew we were not yet out of the fire. After perhaps thirty minutes we happened upon a dry riverbed. It appeared on my map so I was expecting to see it. It was about fifteen metres wide and a couple of metres deep at its centre, with steep banks on both sides. There was no way of boxing it so we would have to cross, taking our chances in the open ground. I used the binoculars to scout along the riverbed in both directions and see if I could spot any enemy. All appeared clear. Contrary to what we had been doing all this time, the move across the riverbed would be done quickly and in a tight group. Crossing the obstacle at speed and as one would lessen the chances of our being shot at should we be seen.

On my command we broke cover, sliding down the bank before making the dash for the other side. Just as we were scrambling up the far bank the air was suddenly filled with machinegun fire. We were sprayed three or four times with long bursts. I remember the ground exploding all round me. I was up and into cover with Stu hot on my heels. Richard cursed as he clambered frantically over the lip of the bank. He'd been hit. I told Stu to move away from the shooting while I pulled Richard into cover. Bullets were coming in thick and fast, slicing through the scrub and cutting branches all around us. Fortunately the ground banked away fairly sharply, putting it between us and whoever was doing the shooting. We moved quickly until we were well into the lee of the slope. Now that we were relatively safe I stopped and asked Richard to tell me where he had been hit. He had taken a round below the right knee. I pulled my knife and cut his trousers. I had a quick look. Thankfully it appeared to be a flesh wound. I quickly slapped a field dressing onto it then asked Richard if he could walk. He was adamant that he would be okay to move. If the bullet had hit bone then we would have been forced to carry him out as best we could.

We could stay here no longer. The machinegun was hammering away, rounds stitching wildly through the scrub in search of us. We would follow the lay of the land, keeping the incline between us and the enemy for protection. I told the others to follow me. We kept moving as fast as we were able, until we were clear of the immediate danger. Turning north once more we cut away for about five hundred metres until I called for a halt.

I checked Richard's dressing to make sure it hadn't worked loose. It was heavily bloodstained but holding firm. Richard was in obvious pain but insisted he could keep going. I did another map appreciation and managed to figure out our position in relation to the firm base. We weren't going to go for that now. We couldn't possibly endanger the Chris' team.

I knew Freddie would be converging on the area with all speed and in as much force as they could muster. We'd got to put as much distance between them and us as possible. Onwards we moved, as fast as Richard's leg would allow.

It was now some thirty minutes since the contact. We stopped again and I checked Richard's dressing. I told Stu to get on the radio and send a brief situation report to the firm base. Frustratingly it took him some time to establish a voice link. He told them what was happening and warned that they should leave their position and move away from the FRELIMO activity before they found themselves caught up in it. I also issued the codeword which would launch a 'hot extraction' mission. The theory was that the RhAF would have a chopper on standby to launch a rescue mission for patrols operating behind enemy lines. Once the codeword was received, the chopper would fly directly to whoever made the request, or to a prearranged rendezvous point. Like I said, that was the theory. Often there were no helicopters available, especially if Fireforce missions were in progress. We were about ten kilometres from the RVP. It would have been great had we had the ability to guide a chopper onto our location. We could have done so but for the fact that I knew we could no longer rely on our radio's battery. Hopefully, our giving an ETA at the rendezvous point would allow the chopper to meet us. It was a one shot trick. If we didn't get there in time the chopper would leave and we would have no means of recalling it. I had hopefully shortened the odds by giving our time of arrival as three and a half hours from the time of transmission. Despite his wound Richard was going well. We weren't going to piss about now. We would get to that bloody RV point come hell or high water….

We were on the move once more. There was now no doglegging, we were heading straight for our destination. Behind us Freddie was approaching. We could hear vehicles and the occasional gunshot. Whilst I remained confident that the Freddie's on foot wouldn't catch us, for those riding on vehicles it would be a different matter….

We were still going at almost jogging pace. The only thing holding us back was Richard's leg wound. Stu and I had emptied the contents of his pack into our own in order to lessen his load, but it now appeared to be having little effect. He reported that his leg had swollen and stiffened and he was having great difficulty putting weight on it. We stopped briefly to allow me to examine the wound. He was right, his leg had swollen and as a result the field dressing was dangerously tight. I Prompted Richard to take some water and a couple of salt tablets. Lifting the dressing away opened the wound and it began to bleed profusely. As quickly as I was able, I slapped a clean dressing onto it and tied it off as loosely as possible. Poor Richard was in great pain but he remained adamant that he could move under his own steam. We were really going to be screwed if he couldn't go on. There was no way we would abandon Richard, so Stu and I would have no alternative but to carry him.

Behind us, the noise continued. Whistle blasts and vehicles, but no shooting. The FRELIMO trucks didn't appear to be closing, which was a great relief. I can only presume that, fearful of possible ambush, they were crawling along at walking pace so that the main body of troops could keep up with them. I wondered if the MG team who engaged us had given a description. Surely they must have told someone that there were only three Rhodesian soldiers?

We had to get to that bloody RV point before the helicopter was due to arrive. We had about two hours left. If Richard's leg held out, we could just do it....

Onwards we toiled, our pace steadily decreasing as Richard found it increasingly difficult to walk. We were passing through fairly open country and had been moving on a steady bearing for all that time. Our efforts to anti-track were virtually nonexistent because we had been prioritising speed above all else. Given how Richard was moving it would have been all but impossible for him to cover his trail anyway. Any Freddie tracker would have had a very easy time of following our spoor. Also, it wouldn't take a genius to work out our direction of travel. If one on the FRELIMO officers engaged his brain then it would be simplicity itself to put some vehicle borne troops ahead of us and ambush us when we appeared.

Quite by chance we happened upon a game trail. Trails such as this are a common sight in the African bush; wild animals use them to move to and from watering holes and such. It was well worn and the earth compacted almost like concrete. Deviating from our line of march for a short distance along the trail would throw many trackers off the scent long enough to allow us to open up a decent lead. We approached the trail as if we were going to cut away to the right but once on it we about turned and made our way in the opposite direction.

We followed the trail for about 150 metres before turning off towards the RV. I was most careful to disguise the fact, making sure we left no boot prints or disturbed foliage in our wake for the first ten metres or so. It was then back to the task at hand.

I was beginning to worry. We had fallen behind schedule. Richard was having great difficulty moving at anything beyond a slow walking pace and there were still a couple of kilometres to travel. It would be just our bloody luck if the chopper came in on schedule and missed us! Most other times we could almost guarantee that there would be a hold up, either the G car would had been deployed on other duties or grounded due to weather or technical issues. However, on this occasion, I was willing to bet a month's pay that there'd be no such hold ups. I hoped that should we not arrive in time, we may just be able to squeeze enough juice from our depleted battery to make radio contact on the emergency frequency and call the chopper onto our location.

The G car crew knew that the LZ would be marked by a purple smoke grenade and that the troops on the ground were friendly by virtue of the fact they were wearing their c*nt caps inside out to display the Day-Glo orange ID panels which were sewn into the lining.

As an alternative, and insurance against our radio not working, would it be wise to split the patrol, with either Stu or myself going forward to the RV while the other remained with Richard? It made sense for me to go. Battery permitting Stu could use the radio to guide the chopper onto their location. If the radio was dead, as an alternative he could use his own smoke grenade.

We had a quick discussion and decided that I should strike out for the RV on my own so that we were certain to be there upon the choppers arrival. Instead of simply waiting, Stu and Richard would continue to make their own way to the RV at Richard's pace. Who knows, if there were any delays with the chopper, then they could well arrive before it turned up.

I was loathed to split the patrol but there was just no other credible alternative. We set the RV as an ERV so we could reunite if the chopper was a no show.

The sound of the FRELIMO follow up appeared to have waned, well at least the sound of vehicles anyway. We had no idea if Freddie was still pursuing us on foot, but had to presume so.

I took a couple of swigs of water from my near empty canteen then set off. I was jogging now and determined to make the RV in good time. I had my rifle at the ready just in case I ran into the enemy or an aggressive wild beast.

I finally reached the RV with fifteen minutes to spare. Save for the usual noises of the bush, all was quiet. After tucking myself into cover, I settled down to wait….

Aside from it never arriving, there was no way I could determine if the chopper had been dispatched. That being the case, we were unable to reschedule the operation because of our radio situation. Even if we'd had a fresh battery, our small means did not possess the range to contact Rhodesia. I mulled over the alternatives. Perhaps, just perhaps, we could get through to Chris and his team. They were still on the ground and hopefully within small means range. For that plan to work, they had to be listening in on the emergency frequency though, and the chances of them continuously monitoring it were now slim. If we could somehow make contact, then we might be able to request another extraction at a second location.

It was all wishful thinking. I had to work to the assumption that we were stranded and plan accordingly. We were seventy klicks inside enemy territory. In his current state Richard could not possibly hope to reach safety on foot. Our only hope was to close on a road then hijack a passing vehicle and drive it to the border. That plan wasn't without its dangers but it was all I could think of….

The distant thwack of rotor blades drifted to my ears. I was up, scanning the sky to the west. The heat haze was distorting the view but I managed to pick out a black shape among the rippling light. I turned my c*nt cap inside out so the ID panel was showing then reached for the smoke grenade. I could see the chopper clearly now. It was a bloody Alouette! The Bloody good RhAF bastards!

The crew knew we had no radio comms; Chris made everyone aware of that. Subsequently they were on the lookout for purple smoke. The chopper was about five hundred meters away when I pulled the pin and tossed the canister into the edge of the clearing. Breaking cover, I waved at the approaching G car. Dense purple smoke was billowing as the Alouette made its run in. It touched down in a maelstrom of dust about ten metres away.

Taking off my hat so that it didn't come off and get drawn into the engine, I waited for the pilot to give me the thumbs up to board. As soon as I got the signal I raced forward and clambered gratefully into the back of the chopper, taking the spare seat next to the pilot. Thank the fucking lord for the RhAF! I got the headset on as the Alouette made a vertical takeoff and began to direct the pilot towards the others.

It turned out that Stu and Richard weren't all that far behind. In fact they were less than a kilometre away, passing through the same area of open ground which I travelled. Homing in on the sudden plume of purple smoke, the pilot landed the chopper close to where Richard and Stu were waiting. As soon as they were aboard, the pilot wound up the throttle and made a short rolling take off. We were up and turning for home. I looked at my two mates and they looked at me. We'd done it!

The ambulance was waiting when we arrived at the FAF. Richard was taken aboard it and driven off to the nearby civilian hospital. Later on that same day Stu and I were returned to Hot Springs.

Tired and filthy, we were ushered in to see Lieutenant Bentley. He wanted to know what had happened. We told him the story. After we were dismissed we retired to our quarters (a tent) to discover that Chris and the others had not yet returned.

The firm base boys turned up the next day. Heeding my advice, they had left their position and moved westward, putting themselves beyond the fringes of the FRELIMO search effort. Because the only Alouette the RhAF had available at that time was allocated to rescuing my team, Chris' boys had to wait for it to be turned around before it was sent to collect them.

We never got to know the story of what happened during or after the initial contact, but we guessed that at least two companies worth of FRELIMO were used in the operation to hunt us down. As for ZANLA, no doubt they would have dispersed to avoid air attack as soon as it was realised their camp had been discovered. Regarding the road watch, we had unearthed little of value. Yes the terrs were using the road network, but not in the volumes we hoped. Whether or not there was any follow up as a result I do not know. Perhaps a couple of the dirt roads were mined, perhaps not....

***

I had a bloke by the name of Paddy from HQ drafted in to cover for Richard. Richard himself was recovering in hospital after successful treatment of his wound. Thankfully it turned out that he had sustained relatively minor damage to the soft tissue and would be up and about again before long. Until his return the rather lethargic Paddy would fill his position. I determined at once that Paddy was the typical HQ soldier. Although he had combat experience, he had long become accustomed to shuffling papers instead of handling a rifle. His personal fitness levels were wanting, not surprising seeing he had been polishing chairs with his arse for the past eighteen months. To be honest I wasn't impressed by him in any way.

We returned to Fireforce duties. After a couple of days the whole Troop was called out to deal with a ZANLA unit which had been discovered by one of the recce teams in a dry river valley not far from the Mozambique border. We were given a quick briefing which gave an estimate that the terrorist gang was approximately forty to fifty strong. To get the whole of the Troop on the ground in one go would mean using several Alouettes when there were none available so, given those circumstances and the urgency of the deployment, we would be moved by Dakota and parachute into the target.

We went in low, no more than 400 feet, and were dropped among an area of scattered trees. The fact that we were going in among such obstacles wasn't the best of starts but, to add to our difficulties, the DZ was 'hot' (under fire). The jump itself was nothing more than a blur; I could hear much gunfire as the roar of the ParaDaks engines receded. A couple of K cars had already entered the fray, hammering away at the unseen terrs. I was frantically attempting to steer away from the nearest tree and only just avoided crashing into it. However, my pack wasn't as lucky, getting snared in the uppermost branches where it was most difficult to retrieve. I landed with an almighty thump. At first I thought I had injured myself but quickly realised I was just winded. Bullets were zipping past all over the place as a couple of LMGs swept the drop zone. Struggling out of my harness, I grabbed my rifle and dived for cover. I could see there was little chance of pulling my pack to the ground so abandoned it. I was wearing my webbing and it contained enough loaded magazines for the task at hand.

We had come down in a tight stick so regrouping was no issue. Moving forward in a skirmish line, it was quickly obvious that the two machineguns were being supplemented by men with rifles. The terrs were putting an effective pattern of fire down on us and seemed determined to stand their ground. As if in illustration of the volume of incoming, one man was hit in the stomach and our Troop Sergeant, a bloke called 'Ackers', got a bullet graze across the back of his hand.

We leapfrogged forwards, with our own LMGs in support, until we were within fifty metres of the enemy. The gooks were still unwilling to yield and returning fire with some determination.

The terrain was a mixture of elephant grass and trees, interspersed with rocks and patches of low lying scrub. I was on the ground on my stomach, giving supporting fire to our LMG gunners as they made their run forwards when I spotted a terr. He was hiding behind a tree and popping out to shoot without really aiming. I drew a bead on the point where I expected him to show himself. A couple of seconds later he appeared and I shot him. I then saw another gook. He was crawling low on his hands and knees to the front of where the main body of terrs were positioned. I killed him.

As we closed to where we could fight through, the terrs suddenly seemed to have a change of heart and began to fall back in some disorder. We kept up our shooting. They disappeared into an area of tall grass. We couldn't see the gooks now but kept firing to maintain the pressure. One of the K cars had come in over our lines and was pumping cannon shells into the grass at targets none of us on the ground could see.

We were loathed to go into the grass to flush out the terrs as we would not be able to see beyond a metre in any direction. Also, if it caught fire (which, with all the tracer rounds zipping about the place, was a distinct possibility) we may find ourselves trapped. Bentley must have realised the danger, he ordered two Sticks to go firm and the remaining two (of which mine was one) to move out onto the flanks and encircle them.

By now the terrs were making a break, some of them ran into the recce stop group and were cut down. Almost as soon as we got onto the right flank we encountered four or five terrs skulking in the scrub. We opened up on them and Paddy the desk jockey killed one before they disappeared into cover. Shortly afterwards we lobbed a brace of frag grenades into an area where we suspected more terrorists were hiding. They exploded and we heard screaming. That was it. A sudden calm descended over the scene. The surviving terrs shouted in English that they wanted to surrender. Ackers told them to come forward slowly with their hands up and they did. There were about a dozen of them altogether and some were walking wounded. They were sat on a patch of open ground and searched.

After we had secured the area the K cars flew off in search of escapees. We had killed nine of the bastards and wounded and/or captured another twelve. That meant there were possibly up to thirty one gooks sprinting for Mozambique. We didn't have the resources to interdict them so, unfortunately, they got away. After we searched the bodies for items of potential intelligence value and gathered the abandoned weapons, we prepared for the wait to be recovered by chopper.

***

I got some leave but was thrown back into the thick of things upon my return. A detachment from the Rhodesia Regiment had set up temporary home at our base to provide support while we busy doing Fireforce and recce duties. The RR guys were out and about on the ground, giving protection to civilian convoys and carrying out other important tasks.

ZANLA continued to penetrate our porous eastern border and had stepped up their mine laying programme. The frequency of attacks upon soft targets was also on the increase. There was one instance whereby ZANLA attacked a missionary school and butchered all the white nuns and priests who were teaching the black pupils. A few civilian buses had also been shot up and passengers murdered. It seemed that ZANLA was popping up all over the place only to disappear before we could get our hands on them….

My Stick was put back across the border a few nights after my return to duty. On this occasion we had been tasked to lay mines along parts of the road network which ZANLA and FRELIMO were using to ferry Rhodesia bound terrorists and supplies.

We were inserted by chopper – in fact it was one of the recently acquired 'Cheetah' helicopters, better known as the Bell 205 of Vietnam war fame. It was the first time any of us had seen a Cheetah, let alone ridden in one. We had our usual extended patrol kit plus a dozen anti-tank and some anti-personnel mines. They were heavy and we had them slung under a Mopani pole for ease of transport.

We moved the ten kilometres to our LUP, a scrap of high ground which overlooked the road which was to be our target the following night. The road itself was of the usual dirt 'construction' and lay about 600 metres from our position. We had a good view with the binoculars and could see at least a couple of Ks along it in both directions.

The first day passed slowly. We mounted a road watch to ascertain just what, if any, ZANLA and FRELIMO traffic was passing along it. Not long after sun up the first vehicles appeared. If my memory serves me correctly, over the course of the day we counted some forty vehicles, most of which were travelling towards Rhodesia. The majority were of the RL type, with flat beds and canvas backs. We couldn't see what they were carrying, which was most frustrating, but we knew it would either be men or supplies. Tellingly, they were all driving normally. Had they any inkling that mines may have been laid, it would have been a different story.

After dark we set out for the road. Frank and I were going to lay the mines, while Stu and Paddy provided cover. We arrived at the target in good time but were forced to wait until the early hours because a couple of small convoys (totalling some eight trucks) passed along the road. The road was wide enough to handle two way traffic and well used. The ruts worn into the dirt were hard and it was into them where we would insert the AT mines. Very carefully, I dug out a section from one of the ruts used by Rhodesian bound traffic and placed the spoil onto a small canvas groundsheet. I then laid the anti-tank mine – into which I had already inserted the fuse – and, after removing the safety I backfilled the hole with topsoil taken from the scrub. My aim now was to blend the hole into the surrounding rut so that it could not be seen. There was no issue about running my hands over a live mine. It was pressure sensitive but required objects of a certain weight to trigger it. I could have safely stood on it without fear of it exploding (I never tested that theory though!). For a vehicle, exerting the necessary kilograms per square centimetre, it would be a different story.

While I was at my own task, Frank was busy seeding both sides of the road with a few anti-personnel mines. These were small devices of the 'bounding' variety. Basically, when initiated, a bounding mine sends the main charge up into the air where it explodes at about chest height. Packed with ball bearings, the mine sends a shower of bearings out across a 360 degree arc. Anyone standing within fifteen metres is almost certainly killed. Ours were rigged up to tripwires to increase their chances of being detonated.

The idea was that once the first truck in a convoy had been taken out by my mine, the others would come to a halt. Thinking they might come under attack, whoever was riding the trucks would bundle out and scatter for cover in the scrub. If they did, they would run straight into Frank's little presents. We were determined to maximise the effects of our mines and kill as many terrorists as possible so this was a neat dirty trick.

Once we satisfied ourselves that our mines were sufficiently camouflaged we moved off. We emptied the spoil from the hole out where it wouldn't be found before following the road to a small junction and placing a couple of AT mines there.

ZANLA, supported by FRELIMO, were more than happy to lay mines on Rhodesian roads so we were playing them at their own game. However, unlike the terrs, we weren't indiscriminate. Of course our mines couldn't differentiate between civilian and terrorist traffic, but we had positioned them in an area where we knew only FRELIMO or ZANLA vehicles were passing.

We moved off to our second LUP some five kilometres west. Over the next two nights we laid the remaining mines along the local road network.

We had been expecting a resupply of mines but instead were told were to be extracted and warned of radio intercepts which indicated that Freddie suspected Rhodesian saboteurs were still in the area and were in the process of initiating a mission to search for them.

Before departing for the helicopter RV, I decided to leave a parting gift for FRELIMO. We deliberately cut away from our LUP in the opposite direction to our real destination, leaving spoor in our wake. Within a short space of time we happened upon a small flat rock. Lifting it we each took a piss then dumped a split tube of cheese (yes, you read that correctly – cheese in a tube! Oh the joy of Rhodesian army rations!) into the area beneath the rock. The hope was that a FRELIMO tracker would get onto our false trail and spot the flies which by then would be crawling all around the rock. Being switched on to such small signposts, the tracker would lift the rock in the belief we had dumped something under it. From what was found he guessed he could possibly get more clues about the Rhodesian patrol. However, upon lifting the rock he would trigger the frag with its instant detonation fuse which we had carefully wedged underneath. It was hoped that it would kill the tracker and anyone standing close by.

Upon our arrival back at base we were informed that a FRELIMO truck had run over one of the mines we laid on the first night. The truck and its cargo had been destroyed and its driver killed. Just as we suspected, thinking that they were being ambushed those following on behind had bailed out then fled into the bush where they ran slap bang into the AP mines. FRELIMO radio traffic reported that in total five men had been killed and nine wounded. Another truck, this time one of ZANLA's, had also been destroyed when it hit another mine laid near the junction. Our intelligence people had no firm details, but they knew the truck was carrying ammunition. Freddie had been forced to stop all traffic while he swept the roads for mines. I can only presume that they found the others but we had fitted them with anti-lift/tamper devices. I guess that Freddie may have lost one or two of his EOD men as a result.

This was a good tactic and a cost effective way of interfering with the terrorist's strategic mobility. To have main supply routes disrupted, even for relatively short periods of time, was bound to have a detrimental effect upon ZANLA operations. As for Freddie, we were tying up resources which he chronically short of. EOD specialists were very thin on the ground and to kill a few of them would do our cause no harm.

Over the following few weeks the Troop was fully committed, carrying out Fireforce and recce patrols. My Stick went back across the border to seed anti-personnel mines along the network of footpaths which led from Moz to Rhodesia. Again, we not only mined the paths but the brush to either side in the knowledge that the terrs would instinctively break and run for cover in the event of an explosion. The tactic of mine laying was paying dividends, with intelligence reports stating that ZANLA were becoming nervous about using their traditional infiltration routes for fear of running into mines.

***

A fully recovered Richard returned to the Troop and a much relieved Paddy went back to REMF duties. I am perhaps being too harsh on Paddy. He was a decent soldier and generally a good bloke. I guess it wasn't his fault that he was more suited to pen pushing than active service. The bare bones of it were he had been asked to do more than he could deliver. He hadn't trained in recce/covert work like us, but he had gone along anyway without any fuss when we deployed behind the lines on our mine laying operations.

We were moved from the eastern front to a FOB close to the town of Kariba and the lake. Lake Kariba is a massive expanse of water, some 200 kilometres long by (in parts) 50 kilometres wide. It formed a natural border between Rhodesia and Zambia. At our end was the Kariba dam, a massive structure which supplied hydro-electrical power to the Rhodesian grid and beyond. At the other end of the lake was Victoria Falls – the place where Stanley met Livingston. The whole area was under threat by Zambian based ZIPRA terrorists. ZIPRA had been amassing large numbers of men, including a sizable force of conventionally trained 'infantry'. The threat they posed was serious enough to have all available Rhodesian reserves mobilised and deployed to counter the threat.

Our two Special Forces units, the SAS and Selous Scouts (the Selous Scouts were a predominantly black outfit), were busy behind the lines in Zambia in an attempt to disrupt ZIPRA. The SAS busied themselves demolishing key bridges and destroying railway lines while the Scouts mounted ambush and assassination missions. The RhAF was also extremely active over southern Zambia, conducting numerous strikes on terrorist training and holding camps as and when they were identified. There was plenty going on and we were soon advised that we were about to join the cross border operations.

My Stick was tasked to carry out mine laying along a couple of ZIPRA main supply routes. It was to follow the pattern we had become accustomed to. Insertion by chopper then place mines at night in the hope of disrupting the terrorist's logistics effort.

We were put into what was deemed a 'safe' area (one supposedly devoid of ZIPRA or Zambian army patrol activity). The country was very close indeed, covered in trees and thick scrub, with only the occasional patch of open ground to break up the monotony.

That same night we moved up to the first road and put it under observation. We watched and waited until the early hours, but the traffic did not abate. There were ZIPRA vehicles moving along it all the time and the short breaks in between each convoy left us no time to place an AT mine. If we couldn't dig a mine into position then what could we do? Our mines were pressure detonated so it was imperative they be sited where they would be run over. If we just left a mine on the surface it would be seen and measures taken to remove and/or defuse it before it caused damage. Frank and Stu argued that it was impossible to lay any mines on this road while ever the volume of traffic remained at its current level. They were correct, but only partly. This road was obviously a major artery for ZIPRA, feeding their forward units with reinforcements and supplies which were vital to their plans. With that in mind we could not just walk away and leave it.

My mind had been whirring for some time before I came up with a solution. We set off south – towards the front line – and were scouting for anomalies in the road which I reckoned we may be able to exploit. Though we went to ground each time vehicles passed, we were well in cover and had no chance of being seen by them.

We had gone less than 200 metres when I spotted what I had been looking for. The twin track dirt road was a mass of small undulations. It was in one of these corrugations that I hoped to place a mine. Yes, we had no time to dig but I thought we could still lay and camouflage a mine to the point where it wouldn't be seen in the headlights of vehicles travelling at some speed.

We were all carrying a claymore mine, these were anti-personnel devices used for ambush or area defence. Working within breaks in the traffic, I had Richard and Frank site the Claymores along the tree line starting just a few metres north of where I intended to lay main AT mines. Once the Claymores were in place, linked up and the wire spooled out into the bush, it was mine and Stu's turn.

It was about 0300 now and the traffic still flowed. We had but a few minutes to do the job. We had collected some topsoil from the edge of the road and placed it in a couple of sandbags. I had given Stu detailed instruction on what he should do and we settled down in the brush to fit the fuses and await our chance. While Frank and Richard watched the road for approaching vehicles, we were to take advantage of the first lull in traffic. Running out into the road, we would place the mines in the dips and, after arming them, empty the topsoil on top and spread it out to disguise the mines as best we could in the short time available. It was a crude yet hopefully effective expedient.

About twenty minutes passed before I gave the order to go. Breaking cover, we sprinted into the road and placed the mines. I fumbled before successfully removing the safety then spread the soil. Within three minutes we were back in the embrace of the brush. Even though it had been done in haste, we had managed to blend the soil in with the track, thus rendering the mines invisible. We moved out as far as the Claymore wire would allow. The initiator had already been attached so all there remained to do was lay in wait.

We had placed the mines on the opposing lanes of the road, but were hoping that the one I had placed would be struck first. The southbound trucks would be carrying men or material destined for the front, while northbound traffic was returning to depots after delivering their loads.

We hadn't long to wait. Great! It was a southbound convoy! We couldn't see the road and had our heads down anyway in anticipation of my detonating the Claymores. BOOM! The explosion cut through the night before rolling away into the bush. Even though I was expecting it, I still flinched at the noise. I waited with my hand on the initiator. I heard shouts and the general noise of panic. The four Claymores exploded as one. They had been placed so as to cover about forty metres of road. Instantly, a lethal shower of ball bearings swept the scene, striking vehicles and killing anyone within range. In order to maximise their effect I had waited for the terrs to come tumbling out of the other trucks to see what happened to the one in front.

After pulling in the severed wire we set off slowly away from the area….

All we knew at that time was that we'd definitely destroyed the leading ZIPRA truck. Judging by the voices, it was also a safe bet to assume we had killed and wounded some terrorists. The cumulative effect of the Claymores being detonated in close proximity to the convoy would no doubt have done some serious, possibly terminal, damage to the other vehicles.

This incident alone would cause serious repercussions for the terrs but would hopefully be magnified if the second mine was hit. As with our mine laying efforts in Mozambique, the road would be closed while it was swept for other mines. ZIPRA didn't have any EOD capability, so it would be left to the Zambian army. Their own small cadre of bomb disposal people were stretched way beyond capacity by all the Rhodesian activity elsewhere in the forward areas. I guess the quickest way they had to deal with any unexploded mines was to place a small charge on them and simply blow them up where they lay, but even this required troops who had some specialist training. If anyone attempted to defuse our mine they would have to know what they were about because it had an anti-handling device built into it.

As a result we could safely expect this main supply route to be closed for at least 48 hours while it was swept and the other mine made safe. This timescale was rather generous, and that 48 hours could easily become three or four days. That doesn't sound long, but it meant that the terrs were losing vital supplies and reinforcement at a time when they could least afford to.

The best thing of all was that the mines we were using had all been captured from ZANLA and ZIPRA terrorist gangs, or taken as booty from cross border attacks on their bases. There was a delicious irony in the fact that we were using terrorist weaponry against the people who intended to use it on us!

We moved away from the area and spent the day holed up in good cover. The following night we struck out for the second road. ZANLA and the Zambians would be on full alert now as they knew Rhodesians were operating in the area, so we would have to exercise caution lest we ran into any of them.

We found the road; a single lane dirt highway, to be quiet. We couldn't understand why ZIPRA wasn't passing along it, especially given that the other route would be almost certainly closed. We set about our mine laying, carefully camouflaging each device within the ruts of the track. We expended our supply of mines, laying them along a two kilometre stretch of the road, making sure they were laid at points where a vehicle couldn't go off road to bypass them.

Our work finished, we cut away to the extraction point and waited to be lifted out. I don't know if the second nights mine laying reaped any rewards, but I'd like to think that we caught a ZIPRA vehicle and also forced the closure of that route.

Within a couple of days we were briefed for another job. Instead of mine laying, we were going to attack a target of opportunity on another important ZIPRA main supply route. This road, unlike the others, was a modern highway of tarmac construction. We couldn't dig mines into it, so would mount an attack from the roadside using specially made up charges.

The explosives – C4 plastic – were made up into satchel charges which, in turn, had been adapted for use as roadside ED's. The C4 had been sandwiched between a steel plate and a thick layer of 'shipyard confetti'. This 'confetti' comprised a bucketful of old steel nuts and bolts. The principle behind these devices was as follows. Staked into the ground at the roadside and chain linked with detcord, when a suitable target appeared they would be command detonated. The heavy steel plate would direct the force of each explosion towards the target and the confetti would be hurled out with tremendous force into whatever lay in front. The nuts and bolts would be possessed of enough kinetic energy to wreak havoc among soft skinned vehicles. It was a cheap and very effective solution to a military problem.

We were to employ four of these devices. Because of their weight and that of the detonation gear, we would have no option but to carry them under a length of scaffolding in Mopani pole fashion.

That same morning we were inserted by G car into the wilds of the bush. The Alouette had struggled to become airborne and I guessed it was perhaps exceeding its stated load. The mines weighed in at about 15 kg each, and then there were the four of us, our personal equipment and the detonation gear plus the two crew members. Although I have no evidence with which to back up my theory, I presume as a result of the combined weight of its payload, the chopper handled like a brick.

We moved through the bush, taking it in turns in pairs to carry the heavy 'Mopani' pole. We arrived at our LUP in the afternoon and settled down to watch the road. Our LUP was on a piece of high ground less than a hundred metres from the target highway and we enjoyed good views along it in both directions. We noted with much satisfaction that the brush and scrub extended almost to the very edges of the road. This was great news, as it meant we could place our charges in cover where they couldn't be seen. Our main problem was the actual detonation itself. We had no way of remotely exploding the charges, so it would have to be done via a wire by someone physically pressing a button. The person initiating the explosion would not be able to see the target as it passed, therefore was unable to detonate the charges at the point where they would do maximum damage. We had thought about this while back at base and had requested a couple of walkie talkies from the stores. We were surprised to be given some made for civilian use. They were quite compact, with telescopic aerials. Even in the best operating circumstances, they were good for no more than a kilometre. That last point wasn't an issue as we knew we wouldn't be using them at ranges more than three hundred metres. The plan was to split into two teams of two. Team one would remain at the LUP while team two would be responsible for exploding the charges. Team one would instruct the others as to exactly when to press the exploder before team two returned to the LUP.

After dark we moved to the roadside and began to set the charges. There was little finesse about it. It was simply a case of making sure the steel plates were at the rear then spiking each of the devices firmly into the ground. We used a hammer to drive three metal rods into the earth to hold each of the charges in place. Although this created noise, there was nobody about to hear it. We set them at ten metre intervals and finished off by linking them together with detcord. The fronts of the charges were convex. As a result, when they went off they would spread the 6kgs worth of shipyard confetti contained in each one across a shallow arc. The way we had positioned them meant each arc was interlocked so we had an area of road covered which extended to more than fifty metres. Even if a convoy was well spaced (which our observations the previous day suggested it wouldn't be) we would catch the first three vehicles in a broadside of shrapnel.

We retired, spooling out the wire and connecting it to the exploder. Stu and I returned to the LUP, while Richard and Frank stayed behind to initiate the ambush.

The next day we watched and waited. There was a steady build up of traffic going in either direction but, as I mentioned previously, we wanted to hit vehicles which were heading towards ZIPRA forward bases, that way we could be guaranteed to maximise the effect of our action.

Vehicles came and went and we let them pass. We were looking for an obvious ZIPRA convoy. Just after noon I spotted a potential target. Seven trucks, all canvas backed, heading towards the border. They were being driven at some speed and were nicely bunched up. I had already tested the walkie talkie to make sure we had comms and passed a warning to stand by to Richard. I knew we'd have to time it well. Richard had the walkie talkie in one hand and the exploder in the other. As soon as he heard me say 'fire' he would press the button and within a millisecond the charges would detonate. For my own reference I had a tree growing at the roadside as an aiming point. I knew that when the lead vehicle drew level with the tree, it and most of the others would be within the blast zone.

"FIRE!" There was a tremendous boom. The dust threw a curtain over the scene for thirty seconds or more. When it began to clear I could see some of the damage. The lead truck had rolled on down the road a little before coming to a halt. The following two trucks had veered off the road and into the scrub. Truck number four had also been hit, but perhaps not as badly. The last truck appeared to have escaped the blast unscathed. Looking through my binos I could see that the first three vehicles were peppered with holes from the confetti. Flat tyres and smoke issuing from one of them confirmed it was well and truly dead. I saw no movement in or around the trucks but knew that any survivors would flee in terror into the bush and run into the bounding AP mines we had also placed in order to catch them. I concluded that the vehicles were carrying freight as opposed to terrorists and I was slightly disappointed that I hadn't been able to kill a few truckloads of the gook scum.

One of the trucks suddenly caught fire. Bright orange flames and oily black smoke drifted skywards. No sooner had Richard and Frank returned to the LUP when the air was suddenly rent with a cacophony of explosions. The staccato firecracker pops and bangs told us that ammunition was cooking off in the back of the blazing truck. So that answered one puzzle, at least one truck was carrying a resupply of ammo. Now the gooks would be a little lighter on AK47 bullets.

By this time the last truck had turned around and driven away from the scene. We could have opened fire on it but that was a waste of time, only serving to tell the enemy where we were and allowing a Zambian follow up. None of the AP mines had gone off, but they would wait their turn, hopefully being tripped by those who arrived to investigate what had happened.

We arrived back at our Kariba FOB the following day and went through the usual report writing/debriefing stuff.

The combined activities of the Rhodesian military inside Zambia was beginning to have a real impact upon the terrorists. They were now unable to provide their forward bases with the logistical support required to maintain their fighting effectiveness. ZIPRA had been in the advanced stages of preparation for a full scale conventional assault on Rhodesia, but not their plans began to stall. Not only were we causing serious disruption to the terrorist's lines of communication but were also attacking their front line units where ever they were found. The RhAF were particularly active, mounting airstrikes against holding camps throughout the forward area and beyond.

Only a day after our return Chris and I were summoned to see Lieutenant Bentley. He had another job for us. Two Sticks, Chris' and my own, were to be inserted into Zambia the following night. The bones of the operation were as follows. Rhodesian troops had quickly established themselves as the 'bogey men' among ZIPRA and their Zambian supporters. To spook them even further and give the impression that large numbers of Rhodesian soldiers were operating inside Zambian territory, we were to mount an ambush on a ZIPRA vehicle column travelling on an important road some way north of our usual area of operations. The hope was that both the terrs and the Zambian military would be fooled into thinking we were ranging far deeper beyond the border area than had first been suspected. The ruse would also probably tie up precious Zambian army resources which would be better employed elsewhere.

There were eight of us, for the trick to work we would have to make ourselves appear as if we were at least Two Troops strong. To that end every other man was issued with a Russian made RPD drum fed LMG which had been liberated from the terrorists at one time or another. Four such weapons, spread out along the firing line, would quickly make the enemy think he was being attacked by a large force. We also considered taking an RPG, but finally decided against it (the RPG was another non standard issue weapon, but many examples had been captured from the terrorists and put to work by the Rhodesians against their former owners).

It was to be a quick in/out job. We were to be dropped by parachute, spending as little time on the ground as possible before being exfiltrated by a Cheetah helicopter. Intelligence reports indicated that the highway – a wide tarmac road which handled two-way traffic – was always busy and a preferred route for ZIPRA convoy movements. Bentley told us that the best time to hit the enemy would be early evening as we would then have plenty of time to make our getaway under cover of darkness. That said he did stress that, regardless of time, it was up to us to initiate an ambush if we saw a particularly juicy target.

Bentley, Chris and I went over aerial photographs. There was a low rise running parallel to and about 150 metres from the road. If we took up position there we would be afforded a commanding view over the target and beyond. Bentley assured us that the ambush point was far enough away from the nearest Zambian army base to allow us to withdraw without fear of compromise.

The ambush was to play out as follows. We would lay a large command detonated explosive device, similar in construction to those we had used on our last job, at the roadside and trigger it when the lead vehicle of our chosen target drew level. The hope was to stop the front truck and cause the others to come to a halt. Once stopped, we would open fire, spraying the rest of the convoy with LMG and rifle fire. The aim was to destroy the vehicles and their contents and kill as many terrorists as possible. Those who remained would have only one possible escape route, but fleeing into the bush on the far side of the road would see them run into the AP mines we had laid there to trap them.

In the end I decided to take an RPD, bringing the total up to five, and three 100 round drums. We were wielding plenty of firepower and were confident of our ability to wreak havoc on the terrorists….

The following night we deployed. The ParaDak flew a circuitous route in order to confuse the Zambian radar operators. Zambia boasted a modern military radar and air defence network which the RhAF had to be wary of. To lessen the chances of it being noticed that the Dak was dropping paratroops, after we had gone the Dak was carry on to a point further north were it would circle for fifteen minutes. The Zambians could interpret this in a number of ways, but the most likely was that the aircraft was acting as an airborne radio relay platform, sending and receiving messages from SAS callsigns who they knew to be operating deep inside the country.

The drop was straightforward and made from five hundred feet. We quickly assembled and set out for our destination some ten kilometres away. We made the move without incident and were settled onto the ridge well before first light.

The road was as busy as Bentley promised. There were frequent ZIPRA convoys moving south towards the Rhodesian border and some of them were very tempting indeed. However, we could do nothing but watch and take notes.

After dark my Stick moved forward to place the roadside bomb and the AP mines. There was no rush. We took our time planting the devices where they would have the maximum effect. Instead of a hard wired set up, the bomb was to be detonated by radio remote control. There were no obstructions between us and it, but just to be sure I ran it on a test before it was connected to the bomb. It worked perfectly.

The following morning came and the traffic soon started to build. We knew that the first convoy we saw which was really worth our attention would be the one we attacked. Regardless of the time of day, we were determined to make the most of our chance to strike at ZIPRA.

We stayed our hand on a few occasions, allowing good targets to pass by unmolested. Both Chris and I were beginning to sweat. In waiting for something which may never arrive had we let the best targets go?

About thrce hours before last light our patience paid off. A convoy of five trucks came trundling along the road. Unusually the canvas backs were down and inside we could see that each one was loaded with ZIPRA! They were all carrying firearms and most appeared to be kitted out in olive green uniforms. We'd hit the jackpot!

Strangely, Chris seemed to hesitate. Including the driver, there was about twenty one men per vehicle. 105 terrs, a whole Companies worth of ZIPRA conventionally trained infantry and eight of us. I could see where he was coming from but I quickly persuaded him that we had to hit this target. It was an opportunity we could not afford to miss. He gave the nod and everyone readied themselves.

I had the exploder and waited for the lead truck to draw level with the aiming point. There were a tremendous flash and smoke and dust followed a millisecond later by a deep bang. I didn't bother spectating as I was grabbing for my RPD. The shooting had already started. Through the dust of the explosion I lined up on the second truck and let fly with two long bursts. Men were tumbling out of the vehicles and scrambling for cover in the scrub. Two or three explosions signalled the fact that some of the bastards had already run into our bounding mines. I put another burst into the cab then switched my aim to where I thought the terrs had gone to ground. Stitching along the scrub line I emptied the rest of the drum and quickly reloaded. Two more explosions in the scrub said that more of the fuckers had tripped our AP mines.

The noise was unbelievable as was the weight of fire. With green tracer rounds from five RPDs zinging all around them, the terrs must have thought they were being attacked by half the Rhodesian army!

My personal mission was to kill as many of the bastards as possible, so I concentrated my fire on the areas of scrub in which I knew the terrs were attempting to take cover. There was some return fire, but not much. The incoming was wildly inaccurate and did not for one minute deter us.

Clipping in my last drum I turned my attention back to the trucks. They had all been pretty well shot up and a couple were on fire. The leading truck – the one which had been caught in the blast – was now little more than a tangled heap of scrap. I smiled coldly when I realised that none of the bastards riding that would have made it out alive.

It was time to go. We'd shot up the terrorist scum good and proper. They didn't know what hit them. Having fired 250 rounds, I'd only about half a drum of ammo left and was guessing the situation was much the same for the other RPD gunners. Those among us who were carrying rifles each had a spare drum with which to replenish us but, even with that, we were dangerously low.

We moved away from the area at speed, leaving the dazed and battered ZIPRA survivors to lick their wounds. Collectively, and including those caught in the initial bomb blast, we calculated that we had accounted for at least forty dead and more wounded. Most of the terrs had been shot down as they attempted to bail out of the trucks. It was fucking beautiful. As I mentioned earlier, it will seem to be extraordinarily callous of me to speak about killing in this way, but these bastards were not fit to live as far as I was concerned. By accounting for as many as possible I honestly felt I was saving Rhodesian civilians from being murdered, tortured and raped. In fact that was the truth of the matter. With every terr I killed I was saving a woman from being raped and butchered, or a family tortured to death. The terrorist bastards showed no mercy and their depravity was boundless, so I had no compunction about ridding the world of them....

We arrived at the helicopter RV point and called in the Cheetah. It arrived about three hours later and lifted us out.

We later learned through intercepted Zambian military radio traffic (our intelligence guys had also cracked their codes) via Bentley that our initial estimates had been accurate. We had killed no less than forty two ZIPRA and wounded another fifteen. This figure included those caught in the initial bomb blast and those who ran into our mines. We had also destroyed the five trucks; a valuable asset which the terrs could ill afford to lose.

It had been a spectacular success and one which exceeded all expectation. It had thrown ZIPRA and the Zambians into a blue funk. They were panicked and dumbstruck in equal measure at the prospect of having Rhodesian troops ambushing ZIPRA in rear areas, areas which up until then had been considered safe. The terrs and the Zambian authorities thought it the work of the SAS, unfortunately we couldn't tell them that they had in fact fallen victim to RLI Commandos....

***

We found ourselves mooching about camp for a few days and living off our stories about the ZIPRA convoy ambush.

Bentley called me into the Troop office and explained he had another job for my Stick. One of the major rivers in Zambia was the Kafue; this body of water separated the bulk of Zambia from the forward areas in which ZIPRA had amassed its conventionally trained 'army'. The SAS had been busy demolishing bridges throughout the area and in so doing had effectively severed another vitally important link in the terrorist logistics chain. In order to counter the Rhodesian actions, ZIPRA had started to put men and equipment across the river in small boats. It was an ineffective and wholly inadequate way of resupply, but nonetheless meant that supplies were tricking through. There appeared to be but one main crossing point and it was that, Bentley informed me, which was to receive our attention.

ZIPRA had established several small holding camps quite close to the Kafue and were moving down to the riverside along a network of footpaths. From there they were being ferried across to join their communist comrades at the Rhodesian border using Soviet supplied rubber boats. Each of the four boats could carry a dozen fully equipped men. Theoretically, ZIPRA could ferry 72 men an hour across the Kafue, potentially in excess of 500 men each night. These figures are my own and no doubt exaggerated, simply because ZIPRA weren't well enough organised to maximise their efforts. That said, it was probable they could be getting around 200 men across with each attempt, so it wasn't quite as ineffective as we might have first supposed.

Bentley pointed out that our target was not the river crossing but the paths leading to it. We were to seed AP mines along these tracks. While it was hoped to disrupt ZIPRA movements, the main aim was to demoralise the terrs and make them feel vulnerable to sudden attack even in areas far behind the front line.

Unusually, Bentley said we were going to go in wearing ZIPRA style uniforms and carrying AK47 rifles (and a patrol RPD LMG). Such things were usually the preserve of Special Forces and, as such, a new one on us. He also went on to explain that because we were operating in such close proximity to areas of population, we were to wear 'black is beautiful' camouflage cream. This simple expedient, when applied correctly to the face and other areas of exposed skin, could make a white man look like a black man.

Although I kept it to myself, my main problem with the mission was the fact that we would be operating on the northern side of the Kafue and thus physically cut off from Rhodesia by the mighty river. At the point where we were to operate the Kafue was approximately two hundred metres wide. While it was fairly slow flowing, it was home to many crocodiles; therefore any attempt to swim the river would result in disaster.

Looking at the aerial photographs which Bentley produced during his briefing, I could see that the area was predominantly open, with a large portion of it turned over to agricultural use.

Bentley went on to explain that, in an attempt to evade RhAF reconnaissance aircraft, ZIPRA was only using the crossing point at night. This would give us a wide window of opportunity in which to lay the mines and clear the area. However, and in order to avoid contact with the terrs, we would have to carry out the mine laying in daylight.

At that point I did suggest that the tracks may well be in use by local civilians. Given the nature of the ground, and the fact that people would be out working the land, after laying the mines we would not be able to remove ourselves from the immediate area without risking compromise….

The operation was delayed as a result of bad weather, so it was a couple of nights before we were inserted by chopper. We were fortunate that it was a full moon and the pilot was able to see well enough to fly in the dark, otherwise we would have been forced to wait until daylight.

Because of the proliferation of Kraals in the area, we were landed some thirty kilometres from the target to ensure the aircraft wasn't heard and reported.

Even though the mission was planned to be of short duration, we were heavily laden. Aside from the usual equipment, we were each carrying trip wire initiated bounding AP mines (which in my opinion were by far the most effective), a spare drum for the RPD and batteries for the big means long range patrol radio. In fact, ever since our little escapade on the hillside in Mozambique, I had insisted on carrying a 'spare' spare battery. My maxim was simple; I'd rather have one more spare and not need it rather than be stuck for want of a battery.

We patrolled to within a couple of kilometres of the target before laying up. We were in cover but could see the flat areas of open ground which surrounded us. There was a kraal about 1500 metres to the north. Worryingly, there was quite a lot of civilian activity within the immediate area. This movement extended from the kraal all the way to our front and consisted of kraals folk tending to crops and animals. It wasn't the numbers (there weren't many of them) but the fact that they enjoyed a virtually uninterrupted view past our current position and all the way to our target. It soon became obvious that the only hope of evading the civvies was to travel along the riverbank. About fifteen or twenty metres from the water's edge, the ground sloped before rising in a shallow bank. The bank itself was only about a metre high, which was not enough to provide adequate cover, but – if we were forced into a rapid move in daylight – it was the only chance we had of not being spotted. This wasn't without its risks though. Crocodiles would often emerge from river to rest on their banks and the Kafue was no exception. Though it may seem implausible, on land a fully grown croc can easily outpace a man over short distances. So, as well as an angry enemy and hostile civilians, if we had to withdraw in a hurry then we would be forced to run the gauntlet of these terrifying creatures….

It was well after midnight when we made our move. We wanted to be absolutely sure that all the civvies were safely tucked up in their huts. It was only a short move, no more than five hundred metres, but we picked our way slowly across the open ground while making absolutely sure we weren't leaving spoor. Our target, the network of tracks leading from the unseen terrorist camps, was well hidden amongst trees, thick scrub and long grass. Although we entered the cover, we didn't want to go too far for fear of bumping into the terrs.

There was some sort of irrigation channel which appeared disused and dry. It was about a metre deep and ran from somewhere in the general direction of the kraal towards the river. We got into it and settled down to wait for daylight.

We could hear voices, singing and the usual clatter of unsecured kit as several parties of ZIPRA passed along the trails to the river. In general the terrs were making a hell of a lot of noise, but I guess they knew they were safe here so far away from Rhodesia and the threat of ambush.

I knew from my briefing that ZIPRA were using four boats. They all had small outboard engines and the zing of two strokes under load ebbed and flowed for several hours as the terrs were ferried across the water to the southern bank.

The activity continued until about an hour before dawn. Having not being able to make the trip, some of the terrs moved back along the trails to their respective camps in the same cacophonous manner as they had arrived.

Bentley told us there were several camps, but that they were all small and well dispersed so as to protect against sudden RhAF attack.

We lay in wait until about noon, listening for any sign of movement. No ZIPRA or civilian passed within earshot or, if they did, they were moving tactically.

Moving from our hide, we made our way through the scrub in the knowledge that it was thick enough to hide us from prying eyes. Our objective was the furthest track. We would lay mines there then work our way back to the start point, seeding the others as we went.

The track was very well used, with the soil compacted and hard. We placed a couple of mines in the scrub to either side of the trail and a little way before the main mine. This last mine was also set into the scrub at a kink in the trail. Like the others, it was heavily camouflaged amongst the undergrowth. The trip wire which would initiate the device was run across the trail and secured at the other side. All the wires we used were almost invisible to the naked eye, even in daylight.

This configuration of mines was deliberate. When a ZIPRA column came along the trail (they would have to move in single file because the track wasn't wide enough to accommodate them any other way), the leading man would trip the first mine. It would bound up to chest height before exploding, killing him and anyone caught within about eight metres of the blast. Those further down the line would instinctively scatter to both sides of the track and initiate the remaining two mines, which were set in a staggered pattern. Combined, the lethal blast radius of the both mines would cover approximately another sixteen metres, giving us the best chance of maximising casualties. Of course the shrapnel would go much further than that, but would probably inflict wounds instead of death.

We systematically worked our way back towards the irrigation ditch. There were four trails in total and we were in the process of working on the final one when Stu, who was on stag, gave a sudden warning. I turned to see a man approaching along the trail. FUCK! He was about fifty metres away. I was the only one out of cover as I had been spooling a trip wire across the trail on the apex of a bend. The bastard had seen me but seemed unconcerned. To him I looked like a ZIPRA comrade. He was dressed in olive green fatigues and a booney hat and had an AK slung casually over his right shoulder. I hissed to the others to hold their fire before waving to the man and then stepping out of his sight round the kink in the trail.

FUCK! FUCK! FUCK! We couldn't let him pass. We couldn't shoot him because the noise would alert everyone in the vicinity. We couldn't spook him into running away for the same reason. I tucked myself into cover and my hand went for my pouch. I had fashioned a garrotte from a length of paracord during basic training and had carried it ever since. I had a fanciful notion that I might be able to dispatch some dastardly terrorist with it once I got into combat. However it had lain unused and little more than a curiosity ever since. Laying my AK aside I readied myself.

Killing someone this way is not like shooting them. Even those the advancing man was a terrorist piece of crap, I suddenly found myself engulfed in doubt. Could I actually do it?

I had no time for further contemplation. I could hear footsteps. At least the bastard had thought nothing of it when he spotted me. Hold on, did that mean there were other ZIPRA about who we hadn't seen?! FUCK! FUCK! FUCK!

The terr rounded the corner. He was a tall, wiry bastard. I was well hidden and he passed me without noticing I was there. I allowed him to take another few steps before I emerged from cover. He must have heard me because he began to turn. I was up directly behind him now and brought the garrotte over his head and round his throat. I remember a blur of movement as his hands went for his throat. I pulled as hard as I could on the garrotte, and brought him backwards and off balance. He went onto the ground on his backside. He was unable to shout, but a strange stomach churning gurgle rent the air. He was struggling like hell but I kept up the pressure, using every ounce of my strength to strangulate him with the paracord.

Finally, after putting up a superhuman resistance, he began to go limp. I held onto the garrotte for a while longer just to make sure he was dead before eventually letting go.

As the man flopped sideways across the trail I suddenly felt quite sick. I suppressed the urge to vomit and softly called the others to me. Stu and I carried the dead gooks body away and dumped it in the undergrowth where we knew it wouldn't be found until after the mines had been tripped. We searched him for anything of intelligence value, stripped him of his ammunition and took the bolt from his rifle. This was a small gesture, but it meant that one rifle was denied to the gooks.

Meanwhile Richard and Frank finished off what I had started with the wire across the track.

We retreated to the 'safety' of the ditch and began to assess the situation. Despite what Bentley told us, ZIPRA was out and about in the daytime. What the fuck had this man been up to? He was on his own, which was a blessing, but would more follow?

It was only about 1600 and we had several hours to go before it fell dark. The local Zambians were still in the fields. If we moved now, even using the riverbank as cover, it was almost certain that we'd be seen.

Would the man I killed be expected back at camp? Would the terrs notice that he was missing? Would they send a party out to look for him? The answer was a probable yes to all these questions. Seeing as he was heading in the direction of the river, ZIPRA may think that he had been attacked and taken by a crocodile. The problem was that once they came looking they would walk into our mines. If that happened in daylight, the fun would really begin….

A couple of hours had passed since our encounter with the gook. Although we were all on high alert, we had settled down a little. Perhaps, just perhaps, our luck was going to hold. As soon as it got fully dark we would be out of here. I had briefed the others on our withdrawal route and set an ERV away to the west should we become split during the move. I had also got Stu to transmit a message back to the FOB, warning them of the situation and the possibility that we may require immediate extraction. By way of return we were advised to clear the area. We replied that it was not possible until after dark as our close proximity to Zambian civilians would result in compromise.

BANG! Shit! Someone or something had tripped one of the mines. From the sound I guessed it was one of those farthest away from our position. Everyone in the vicinity would have heard the explosion and we could be sure that the gooks would turn out to investigate.

We couldn't stay here. We had to move. I thought about going for the bank but the threat of crocodiles and the marginal cover it afforded put me off the idea. No, we would have to move, but we'd strike out across open country. We were all dressed like terrs and carrying terrorist weapons and could easily pass as black men. If we moved across the open ground as if we owned the place, anyone spotting us would assume we were a ZIPRA or Zambian militia patrol.

It was only five hundred metres then we'd be into some cover. Now that we'd divested ourselves of all the AP mines our loads were lightened so we could run if required. But we weren't about to run. After checking our black is beautiful camouflage paint, we made our way westward and soon broke through the brush into open country. Walking as nonchalantly as we were able, we began to cross the farmland.

Behind us we began to hear shouting while over to our right, about four hundred metres away, a few of the kraals folk were watching us as we passed over their property. Just as we hoped, the civvies appeared unfazed and probably took us for friendly forces.

By now we were about halfway across the open area. The shouts to our rear were joined by a few whistle blasts. A couple of gunshots rang out. Telling the others to keep calm I turned to see what was happening. There were a group of about twenty armed men standing on the edge of the scrubland. They were firing into the air to get our attention. That single act confirmed that they weren't sure who we were but were requesting we identify ourselves. I casually raised my arm and waved. I couple of them waved back and I returned to the march.

I reminded the others to play it cool. Once we got into the scrub at the far side of the open area we could run like fuck for a kilometre or so to put as much distance between ourselves and the terrs as possible.

Only a matter of about thirty seconds later we heard a vehicle behind us. I looked over my shoulder to see an old pickup truck driving towards us. There were a few men stood up in the back, they were all hanging on for dear life as the truck bumped and bounced across the uneven ground.

Calling the boys to a halt I quickly explained our next move. We couldn't outrun the truck and when it closed on us the occupants would see through our disguise.

I waved at the truck but its occupants didn't reply. Those in the back were far too busy clinging to anything they could to stop themselves from being thrown out. Casually we had moved line abreast. It must have looked to those in the truck and the others who were still by the scrub, that we were waiting to welcome the vehicle.

"Standby. Standby. Go!"

As one we hit the dirt and opened up on the truck. It was barely a hundred metres away so we couldn't really miss. Frank had the RPD and he let fly with a couple of good bursts. I saw the windscreen shatter and cave in as our rounds struck it. The pickup swerved before coming to an abrupt halt. Those in the back half jumped and half fell to the ground. One was shot dead before he hit the dirt while the rest scattered and ran like terrified hares back towards the scrub line. I saw no one exit the cab so can only presume that both the driver and passenger had been killed.

The unidentified enemy (who I presumed were ZIPRA) were now shooting at us. I told Frank to put some fire down onto them. He responded with a few short, well aimed bursts which caused them to break and scatter for cover.

We were going to fall back in pairs, leapfrogging each other whilst providing covering fire. I'd flicked my AK onto automatic and was putting three round bursts towards the enemy. They had recovered somewhat from their initial shock and were returning fire. I heard an explosion from the scrub. One of the bastards had tripped a mine!

We were withdrawing as fast as we were able. Frank and I running in fifteen metre bounds while the others gave covering fire. We then went to ground and opened up while Richard and Stu ran past us and set up.

Soon, thankfully, we plunged into the scrub. Bullets were still attempting to find us but we were free of the contact.

We ran for about two kilometres, doglegging so as to confuse any trackers as to our direction of travel. When we stopped I got Stu to send a sitrep on the emergency frequency, briefly explaining the situation and requesting that they standby for helicopter extraction.

It was still light and there was plenty of time to go before we could call in the chopper. For a start we had to be sure we had outrun the enemy. By now the Zambians would have mobilised some of their local forces to join the hunt, so we couldn't present them with the gift of a Rhodesian military helicopter which they would attempt to shoot down. No, we had to keep going until we knew it was safe.

We had broken through the bush and were into more open country. Aside from travelling along the riverbank, which none of us wanted to chance, we would simply have to move where we could be seen.

We had only been going for about ten minutes when we spotted another pickup truck. It was heading in our direction and had obviously seen us. Although it was little bigger than a family saloon, the truck was towing a big agricultural trailer – like the ones you would see behind a tractor. Lord knows how they had managed to hook the thing onto the back of the truck. There were a few men standing up in the back of the truck, while on the trailer itself there were at least two dozen men. The noise of the engine told us that it was under enormous strain as it struggled beneath this ridiculous payload. The men were militia types, we guessed they were from the local kraals and had joined in the search. Even above the screams of the engine, we could hear them shouting and whooping. As they closed we could see that most of them appeared to be armed with machetes and knobkerries. As I recall, only four or five of them brandished long arms, most likely homemade shotguns. A couple of the silly bastards had even shown up with bows and arrows!

The truck was managing barely fifteen Ks an hour. I knew they wouldn't have a radio and had no way of telling the main force that they had happened upon us. However, once the shooting started, ZIPRA and any Zambian units would be able to get an approximate fix on the noise and close in.

Make no mistake, despite the comical nature of the militiamen and their transport, they would have hacked us to death had they got their hands on us.

We allowed them get to within 150 metres then we let them have it. They spilled off the trailer and ran like hell, bomb bursting in terror in every direction but ours. Most of them sprinted back towards where they had come. The truck had been hit and abandoned, its driver flinging himself out and away on all fours before joining the great race north. We had killed a couple in our initial volley and wounded two or three more. Abandoned by their friends, the wounded were seen dragging themselves under the cover of the trailer.

I called a halt then told Frank to put another burst into the engine bay area of the truck to disable it for good. It was a good burst, we saw green tracer striking the vehicle where I wanted it to go.

The enemy dealt with, it was now time to go. We set off at a jog, following our bearing westwards towards another area of scrub.

The light was fading now. We were back into decent cover. From our two contacts the enemy would have worked out our direction of travel; however we weren't going to oblige by sticking to the rules and allowing him to head us off.

We soon happened upon a game trail which ran down towards the river. Cutting away north we began to follow the track. Now, just as long as we encountered no other enemy units, we would be lost to the night….

We moved about twelve kilometres north and settled into an LUP from where it was safe to call in a chopper. Stu sent a report on the emergency frequency, passed our co-ordinates then asked for an extraction. We were told that a G car would be dispatched at dawn.

There was a delay, but at around 1100hrs an Alouette appeared, it was flying fast and low over the bush. Stu got on the big means and talked it in. We popped a hand held ground flare which we had spiked into the earth at the northern edge of the LZ. The pilot was watching for this and knew to land immediately south of it.

As soon as the chopper landed we could see it was carrying a drum of avgas in the area we were to occupy. The Alouette was a superb aircraft, but here in the harsh high altitude environs of southern Africa, its operational range was adversely affected. To reach the RV point and get back home again, it would require a refuel. The only way to do this was to carry its own 'spare can'. Once landed, the chopper tech/gunner would use an electric pump to transfer the fuel from the 55 gallon drum into the aircrafts tanks. After replenishment the Alouette would be able to make the journey home.

When we got the okay, I sent Richard and Frank forward to help the tech manhandle the drum out of the aircraft and onto the floor. The refuelling operation was completed in fairly short order and we were told to board.

The Alouette took off and made a five kilometre wide turn south. It was hoped that this manoeuvre would place the aircraft out of small arms range of any follow up units who were still combing the area.

We made landfall back at Kariba without further incident. As far as I was concerned the whole operation had been a waste of time, but Lieutenant Bentley begged to differ. We had succeeded in disrupting the terrs and killing a few into the bargain. Yes they could, and would, simply move their river crossing points, but they did so with the knowledge that they were perhaps being observed and would be attacked. The psychological impact of our mission, and others like it, were extracting quite a heavy toll upon the terrorists morale. They were afraid of ambush and mines even in areas they thought inaccessible to Rhodesian ground troops. They were using resources, resources which would otherwise have been deployed to the Rhodesian border as part of their invasion plan, to guard rear areas and conduct anti-sabotage sweeps.

I did hear, but cannot confirm, that the Selous Scouts sent snipers into these same areas to further harass and disrupt the terrs. By carefully picking off selected targets at long range they were able to deplete ZIPRA of its officers and NCOs, or those specially trained individuals whose job it was to search for and deal with Rhodesian mines.

Sniping activity such as this would produce results totally disproportionate to the meagre Rhodesian resources used. It was said that some of the terrs were deserting, while others refused to carry out security duties for fear of being ambushed, blown up or sniped at. Again, I don't know if that was the case, but it was entirely plausible….

***

During this time, talks had been going on in London. Zimbabwe Rhodesia, as the country was now known, had already held its first ever one man one vote elections under the stewardship of international observers. That election was declared to have been carried out freely and fairly in accordance with international law. The result was that the country now had its first black head of state. Prime Minister Abel Muzorewa was a moderate leader, who had led his own small nationalist movement before moving into mainstream Rhodesian politics.

Under pressure from the British and other powerful members of the commonwealth, as well as the USA and beyond, PM Muzorewa agreed to engage in the Lancaster House talks. For their part, ZIPRA and ZANLA were forced to participate when the leaders of the two countries who had long supplied them with safe havens threatened to withdraw their support. Both Zambia and Mozambique had suffered severe economic damage at the hands of the Rhodesian military and realised that, unless the war could be settled by diplomatic means, the terrorists had little prospect of winning.

The British engineered the talks in typical Machiavellian fashion then steered them towards a conclusion which was good for everyone except Zimbabwe Rhodesia. The basic premise of the final agreement was that we should hold fresh elections in which both ZAPU and ZANU (the political wings of ZIPRA and ZANLA) should participate. Whoever was declared the winner would be recognised by the world community as the legitimate rulers of the new sovereign state of Zimbabwe Rhodesia. The agreement also placed upon its protagonists the condition that they would respect the result of the election.

Getting Abel Muzorewa, Mugabe and Nkomo to sign up to the accord meant that a ceasefire was put into effect. After some thirteen years of brutal conflict, it seemed the bush war had finally come to an end….

We were returned to Cranborne and consigned to depot duties. Meanwhile preparations were being made for the elections. As part of the deal, it had been agreed that our country would revert to British control. A Governor, Lord Soames, was installed as temporary head of state and preparations made for the elections.

Within a matter of days both ZAPU and ZANU had broken the agreement and were allowing tens of thousands of armed terrorists to infiltrate the Tribal Trust Lands and begin a systematic programme of voter intimidation. Dependent upon region, it was made clear that the black population should vote for either Mugabe or Nkomo – or else.

These persistent and deliberate breaches of the Lancaster House agreement were brought to the attention of Soames and his staff, but they refused to act. Only our own government observed the rules during the run up to the election campaign, but our propriety was to cost us dear….

We in Three Commando were placed on general security duties in and around Salisbury and were forced to watch impotently as the

ZAPU and ZANU election machines gathered pace. It was a hateful experience to see terrorists moving openly through our capital. In defiance of every military convention, under strength and under equipped, we had fought these bastards every step of the way. We'd not only fought them but actually rolled them back. We'd killed countless tens of thousands of them and incapacitated many more. We'd suffered grievously in the process of defending our homeland. Civilian atrocities aside, the war had cost us many good men. In fact, proportionally speaking, we had suffered a higher casualty rate than the US during the Vietnam War.

Yes, we had endured many hardships and fought many battles, but we had never yielded. At least our soldiers and airmen hadn't. The same could not be said of our political leadership.

The elections came and went and the winner was announced. Robert Mugabe and his ZANLA communist terrorist thugs had achieved what they could never do by force. They had taken control of Zimbabwe Rhodesia.

In the aftermath of the result many whites fled the country. Property prices crashed and the economy faltered. There was no future for the army, it would be replaced by a new establishment comprised of ZANLA terrorists.

On October the 31st the RLI were disbanded and its colours laid to rest in Salisbury cathedral. I wasn't there to witness the occasion. I had left some time earlier. As soon as Mugabe won the election I realised my future lay outside my country. Whatever the machinations of the new ZANU regime, I knew it would be a question of when, not if, they would turn against the white population.

My aunt had died, so I had no more family connections. I left for South Africa and from there to Europe. Although it was hard for me, my own situation was very easy compared to many of my countrymen. I came from a background of some wealth so had sufficient funds invested in banks outside Zimbabwe Rhodesia to soften the blow. I wasn't exceedingly rich, but I had enough to start a new life in a new country without the constraints which poverty would bring. For thousands of others events played out differently. They found themselves suddenly displaced, penniless and at the mercy of countries who did not want to take them in.

After a few years of itinerant living in several European countries I finally settled in a corner of South East France. My passage into that country had not been without its obstacles, but the fact that I was financially independent eventually meant that I was granted permanent residency.

I bought a smallholding and set to work reinventing myself as a subsistence farmer. Slowly, I began to learn the language, make friends and integrate into French society. I still live there and have a good honest hardworking life. I never married nor had children, but I am satisfied and comfortable with myself and my situation.

I could describe what Mugabe has done to my country but I think that is already evident to anyone who has a reasonable grasp of world affairs. Am I proud of what I did? Yes. Am I troubled by the notion that I killed? No. Would I do it again? Certainly.

I will leave you with one last thought. Don't ever be complacent about your freedoms. They have been bought and paid for with someone's blood. While it is now not usual for political change to occur through war or armed insurrection, it is quite easy for those who do not have your best interests at heart to affect change by socioeconomic means. We should all exercise caution in today's complex and ever-changing world lest we fall victim to oppression by guile….

If you enjoyed this book then
I ask that you please consider leaving
A review.
Thank you.

Made in the USA
Middletown, DE
03 November 2020